WHEN BABIES ARE BORN

EMMA MAI SOWTER

authorHOUSE®

AuthorHouse™ UK
1663 Liberty Drive
Bloomington, IN 47403 USA
www.authorhouse.co.uk
Phone: 0800.197.4150

Published by AuthorHouse 06/12/2018

ISBN: 978-1-5462-9228-9 (sc)
ISBN: 978-1-5462-9229-6 (e)

For my father, who had a vivid imagination and inspired me to write fantasy novels.

I would like to thank all my friends who made helpful suggestions and especially my husband for his encouragement and his help in editing this book.

Part 1

CATHIE'S STORY

Pete and I will always remember the day when our fifteen-year-old daughter, Cathie, announced that she was pregnant and wanted an abortion. Pete reacted very badly to this news and before she could say anything more, he slapped her hard on the face, causing a bruise, a cut lip and another epileptic fit. I'd never seen him so angry before and he'd never been physically violent towards any of us ever. Then, without saying a word, he just stormed out.

Cathie was left lying on the lounge carpet in an unconscious state. To make her more comfortable, I asked Rosie, her twin sister, to help me carry her up the stairs to her own room. As she was only seven and a half stone, this was not too difficult. As we lifted her, her T-shirt rode upwards and her hipsters shifted down, revealing a rash across her abdomen that looked distinctly reptilian.

"What on earth is that?" Rosie asked

"I have no idea," I replied. "Hopefully, we will find out, when Cathie has recovered."

Cathie had been having fits for the past couple of months ever since she had been out all night on a Saturday. At the time, she had told us that she had fallen off her bike and had been unconscious for some hours but this hadn't explained the rope burns and the cuts on her wrists. When she'd not come home that night we'd been sick with worry: so much so that Pete had gone out looking for her on his bike. He'd taken with him a torch and the map she had made which highlighted all the pathways around our village but he hadn't been able to find her. Neither of us had fully believed her story but I'd silently put suitable antiseptic cream on her wounds and bandaged them. Pete had gone out and bought cycling helmets for both of our daughters. Later, I had told Cathie that we would like to hear a more plausible explanation sometime soon but, as yet, nothing had been forthcoming.

When she came around, I took her up some supper and a glass of water.

"Mum," she sobbed. "The pregnancy was not my fault. I was raped! I don't want to talk to Dad about it as he will blame Tom but it wasn't him and I'm ready to tell you the whole story, truthfully as I know it."

"Oh, my dear," I soothed, still not believing her. "You must have been so scared! Why didn't you confide in us before?"

"It's complicated," she said.

"Do you know how far gone you are?" I gently asked.

"I've missed two periods," she replied.

She fished into her underwear drawer and produced two pregnancy testing sticks. I looked with dismay at the two blue lines on both of them.

"Well, it's getting late so shall we wait until the morning? Your Dad may have calmed down by then and I'm sure that he will listen without resorting to violence again."

At the age of fifteen, my girls were beautiful with their long, curly, brown hair and their lovely facial features. They seemed able to eat as much as they wanted without getting overweight. Cathie was in the county trials for gymnastics and it was the same for Rosie but with swimming. She competed in both breaststroke and butterfly just like I had done as a teenager. They were also doing well with their schoolwork, getting 'A's and 'B's like me and not messing around like Pete who hadn't had to work that hard. He'd only really liked Maths, Physics and maybe Geography.

The children had learnt to ride ponies at my riding school but were more interested in their chosen sports which was fine by me. I had told them that they could use Facebook but never to post more than facial images of themselves. I had explained about the dangers to them and about on-line grooming. I thought that they were generally good girls and did what they had been told to do.

With both Pete and I working from home, we were living together as a happy family, in our favourite part of England but Cathie's announcement was about to tear our contented existence apart.

Normally, Cathie was like Pete, outgoing, extrovert and confident. She'd had another boyfriend, before Tom, who was three years older than her. He was called Steve and they'd met at a teen disco. Their first date had been enjoyable. He'd taken her to a reservoir in the family car, to go sailing in his small yacht. He'd told her to wear old clothes beforehand. I'd guessed that this was because she might have fallen in but there had been no such instructions for their second date.

Both she and Rosie had been doing a paper round and Cathie had eventually saved enough money to buy a pretty dress with accessories, which she'd worn the next time they went out. He'd taken her to a woodland area and all seemed to be going well until he'd suddenly grabbed her hand tightly and started to run. She'd fallen over and ended up being pulled through the mud and undergrowth, ruining the outfit she'd saved so hard for and scratching her arms and face. Finally, he'd let go of her hand and just walked away, leaving her to find her own way home.

A few days later he'd called. I'd picked up the phone and inquired, "How could you treat my daughter like that?"

He'd apologised to me and asked to speak to Cathie.

"I'm really sorry for what I did. I don't know what came over me. Would you like to come on another date with my friend Tom and a friend of your choice? We'll be meeting in a pub and I promise I won't hurt you again."

"Ok," Cathie had replied, "But you'd better keep your promise or my Dad will be talking to your parents. He's very angry with you."

After what had happened on their last date, I will never know why she agreed. However, I had been reminded of my own difficulties as a teenager and thought it important to try and be supportive. So, I'd offered to buy her a new outfit which she thought was extremely kind of me and tried to reassure her by saying that she would feel safer with other people around.

Tom had brown eyes and long, shoulder length hair but was not much taller than Cathie and was skinny, with a spotty face. However, he was confident and an extrovert. Cathie and Tom had got on so well that the others left early, as they'd felt like they were being ignored. Cathie was smitten! I think Tom had gone on a couple of dates with her friend after that but, as he didn't seem too keen on her, Cathie had cut her ties with Steve and virtually stolen Tom from her.

Simon, Tom's father, was rich, being a well-known author and the editor of specialist travel and business magazines. He had studied English at Cambridge University. When Tom was seventeen, his father's college at Cambridge had told him that he would only need three passes at 'A' level to follow in his father's footsteps. So, rather like Pete who didn't have to work hard at school, he'd messed around and spent his time socialising. The one problem between them was that Cathie did not come from a wealthy background. Both Pete and I had gone to university but we'd never had that much money. Cathie knew that she had to study hard to get good grades to get into Medicine. Their plan was that she would get into Cambridge too, so they would spend her first year and what would be his third year together. However, he had been unhappy about her choice of subject as he had said that medics had to work too hard. Of course, he was right but she had just not been listening.

Initially, the relationship with Tom had blossomed. Both of them liked seventies rock music and had got on well with each other's friends. To be as honest as she could be, she had told me that she was having a sex life of sorts with Tom. However, she had been adamant that she was not going to lose her virginity until she was sixteen and only then with all the proper precautions. Although this had been a source of frustration for Tom, sex seemed to dominate their relationship, while he was spending a lot of time ignoring her, to go out drinking with his mates.

Pete and I had not been keen on Tom's influence on Cathie but felt that she should have some kind of social life. However, we had been worried that he was ruining her schoolwork. When we had reminded her that she would have to do exceptionally well to get into Medicine, especially at Cambridge, she'd promised us that she would catch up over the summer. Apparently, as part of his gap year, Tom's father had arranged for him to work in Germany during what would be her holiday period. Of course, no-one knew that none of Cathie's plans were going to come to fruition.

Cathie was fast asleep when Pete came back and he was still very angry. Without waiting to hear from either Cathie or me, he took her mobile and phoned Tom's number, asking to speak to his father. Once Simon understood that Cathie was pregnant, he was quite cooperative. He was tired of his son turning up drunk in the early hours of the morning, then playing his psychedelic music, really loud. This would wake the whole household which was especially annoying since his wife, Tom's mother, was dying of breast cancer and Tom didn't seem to care.

Simon and Pete agreed to tell the police who arrested Tom for having sexual intercourse with a minor. Unfortunately, he had been out all night that Saturday and, although there were plenty of friends who would have given him an alibi, they had all been drunk at the time. As Cathie was pregnant, he was forced to take a paternity test. However, while the baby's cells were in Cathie's blood they certainly did not match the sample that Tom had provided. In fact, the pathologist had never seen anything like them before. After the police dropped the charges, Tom phoned Cathie:

"How could you do this to me?" he shouted, "First you get pregnant with someone else when you've denied me and then you accuse me of rape."

"But it..."

"No buts, it's over," he interrupted, "You could have cost me my place at Cambridge!"

Cathie had wanted to explain but he had hung up and she was inconsolable and cried for days. Meanwhile, the rash was growing in size and as the pregnancy was progressing, it was time for Cathie to tell us what had really happened. Through sobs and tears the whole story came out.

It had been a bright sunny day. She'd been cycling down a path away from the swing park which she'd used many times before, as she'd often met her friends there. Both of my twins had cycled all over the countryside around our village from an early age. This had been a source of annoyance and worry for me, as I had wanted them to stay in the close where we lived, especially when they were very young. However, now that they were fifteen years old, I felt confident that they could look after themselves. Cathie's friends had all been away on their holidays and Rosie had been visiting her boyfriend but for some reason this hadn't bothered Cathie as for once, she'd felt like being alone.

Suddenly, she'd come across an old, fairly high gate on the left of the path which was slightly ajar. An overgrown track led away from the gate on the other side and she'd wondered why she'd not noticed it before. She'd got off her bike and left it on the path beside the gate which had swung open quite easily. The first thing she'd come across was a shed that had collapsed as soon as she'd entered it. Having picked herself up and realising that she wasn't hurt, she'd moved on into the rest of what appeared to be a garden.

"Cathie," I interrupted, "I've told you not to explore private property, especially not on your own."

"Well, if you're going to scold me I won't tell you anymore. It's hard enough for me as it is."

"Ok," I said in a softer tone of voice, "I won't, I promise. Please carry on."

The grass was about four feet high and as she'd waded through it she'd come across a disused swimming pool. There was no water in it but it was covered in slime and mould. Turning away from the stench of the pool, she'd realised that the track was leading her to what looked like a dilapidated, deserted house with an open, battered and weatherworn, green door. The paintwork was peeling off the window frames and there was broken glass, presumably from the windows, littered all over the gravel outside. It had definitely looked uninhabited.

However, aware that she might have been trespassing on someone else's property, she'd shouted,

"Hello, is there anybody there?"

There had been no answer.

Pete was still angry, "Get on with it and get to the sex part," he said.

"Shut up and let Cathie tell her story in her own time," I shouted back.

"Well I've got work to do," he said.

"Please stay and listen to her, now that she is telling the truth," I replied.

She'd pushed open the door and walked into the hallway. It was dark inside and dusty. There was a strong musty smell, mould on the walls and what looked like rat droppings on the worn-out carpet. She had been curious enough to open the first door to the room on the left which she thought would have been the lounge but had had to force the door to get in. The room was full of bundles of newspapers. All of them had natural disasters or civil wars as headlines and the plight of the survivors and the distress of the refugees had been highlighted by someone's pen.

Suddenly, she'd felt a strong wind coming through the open doors, shattering more glass in the windows. Then she'd heard a door slamming upstairs. Initially, she'd thought it could just be the wind but then she'd heard a creaking on the stairs. She'd been really frightened and had wanted to run outside but had been rooted to the spot. Had that just been caused by fear or some other kind of power? She'd felt like she was being watched and turned around, without moving her feet, and stared in horror at what she'd seen in the doorway.

The creature was so large that it had filled the space. There had been nowhere to run even if she could have done. Trapped and terrified, she'd wanted to scream but no sound had come out of her mouth. It had said something in a language that she couldn't understand and it had moved towards her, placing its hands on each side of her head. The pain had been excruciating and then there was just darkness as she'd slumped to the floor. When she had regained consciousness, she was alone, lying on a pile of old newspapers. Her hands had been tied together behind her back and her ankles were roped together.

"I felt sore down below and could see blood on my jeans," she wept.

"What did the creature look like?" I gently asked.

"He was covered with reptilian skin and was about twelve feet high, with massive muscles and small red eyes. He had a large nose and an ordinary looking jaw but when he spoke I could see a mouth full of white, sharp teeth. He also had webbed hands and feet, was dressed in military uniform and had a chain of rings around his neck."

Pete gasped and there were tears in his eyes,

"Obviously a megalattan," we both said quietly but simultaneously.

"At least that explains the rash but why didn't you tell us before?" I asked.

"I didn't think you'd believe me and that you would think that Tom had raped me."

"How did you end up being tied up?"

"He must have done it while I was unconscious," she replied.

Later, as dusk was approaching, he'd returned and forced her to eat a disgusting meal. He'd spoken with a thick accent but in English this time.

"I am an ambassador for my race. The food will help your baby to grow tentacles. In the morning, a spaceship will arrive to take you to a safe place. There, you will have my baby and many more. This will be very good for you. You will be highly respected and there will be plenty of other pregnant, human teenagers to socialise with," he'd said.

"My people's planet was destroyed by nuclear warfare which rendered all our females infertile, so we had to dispose of them. Now my people are going to make a magnificent, stronger, hybrid race, combining with humans and you will be part of this venture," he had continued.

Then he'd injected some fluid into the muscle of her arm and said, "This is a humanising vaccine which will make your alien baby change into a normal human, just a short time after being born. Now rest because I will be well-fed and stronger, if you show distress."

She had seen the highlighted writing in some of the newspaper headlines and thought that his race might have caused them but wisely, she said nothing.

She must have dosed off or maybe it was an additional effect of the vaccine because when she'd next woken, it was dark and the alien was asleep beside her on a separate pile of newspapers. A life of giving birth to alien children was a fate worse than death! She wasn't going to give in so easily and had come prepared. There was a small but very sharp, serrated pen knife in her pocket. As quietly as possible, she'd wriggled around until she could retrieve the knife. Having finally got the opened knife in her right hand, she'd started cutting away at the rope around her wrists. It had been impossible not to cut herself and she'd gritted her teeth to avoid crying with the pain. She'd worried that the smell of blood might wake the alien but she was already bleeding into her jeans and what she didn't know was that the alien had a very poor sense of smell.

She'd almost got the rope off when the alien had turned over and briefly opened his eyes but she'd put her head down and pretended to be asleep, so he'd nodded off again. She'd waited about another thirty minutes, until she was sure that he was asleep and then finally freed her hands. Untying the rope around her ankles had been easy and then she'd quietly gone to the front door. Luckily, she'd been able to open it. She hadn't wanted the alien to follow her so she'd then gone back and slit his neck with the knife. Unfortunately, it hadn't killed him, just badly wounded him and, of course, he was now awake.

She'd fled up the path as fast as she could but tripped. Quickly picking herself up, she'd been able to smell him and hear his heavy breathing behind her. However, he didn't or wasn't able to make her stop with his mind this time, maybe as a result of the wound that she'd inflicted. She'd turned and briefly looked. He'd been only a few metres away. She'd had to run like hell to get to the gate but it was locked and she'd not been able to budge it. As she was climbing over it, he'd reached out with an arm and grabbed her foot. For a minute, she'd thought he was going to pull her back down but she'd kicked his hand against the gate until he'd let go. Fortunately, the wound had obviously weakened him and she'd managed to escape. Down on the ground, she'd picked herself up and cycled as fast as she could to get home.

"Mum, your paranoia about cycling all over the countryside and entering peoples' houses is right. I was terrified," she sobbed.

This time the story made sense to us. Cathie would never have known what a megalattan looked like without actually meeting one and neither Pete nor I had described their appearance to her.

"Cathie, I'm so sorry," I soothed and gave her a hug.

Pete said, "I owe you a massive apology. I'm so sorry that I just lost my temper and hit you when you told us you were pregnant. I am mortified by what has happened to you and causing Tom to break up with you. We do believe you now and clearly you must have an abortion as soon as possible. Please believe me that you will have our full support."

Basically, his child had been raped by an alien and was carrying an alien baby which left a bitter taste in his mouth. He knew that his child needed our help.

Although our relationship had been quite strained for ages, I accompanied Cathie to appointments with our GP and then a Consultant in Obstetrics & Gynaecology. With their approval, a date for the abortion was eventually fixed. In the meantime, Cathie had two more fits and seemed to be getting depressed as, at school, her so-called friends didn't want to know her. I felt she should have got some help for this but all my Pete seemed concerned with was getting rid of the baby. The news of alien cells in her blood and a reptilian rash over her skin had somehow been leaked to the press and local newspaper journalists were all over us, when we arrived at the hospital. Fortunately, security wouldn't allow them in.

However, the medical abortion failed! Pete insisted that Cathie should have an operation to remove the baby. The Obstetrics & Gynaecology Consultant advised that, because the baby was alien, there was a significant risk that Cathie could lose her womb. Obviously, this would have meant that she would no longer be able to have children naturally. Despite this, she felt extremely guilty for all the trouble that she had already caused and so readily agreed to have the operation.

The following day, she was brought down to theatre. She had been 'nil by mouth' for hours and was very thirsty. She was given a general anaesthetic and after a normal, pelvic Caesarean cut didn't give birth to the baby, a further incision was made from her ribs to her pelvis. However, the baby had produced thick tentacles, reaching from it into her liver, heart, lungs and gut. The consultant asked a junior, who was not scrubbed in but merely observing, to come out and see us, as we were waiting outside the theatre doors. He explained about the tentacles.

"Do you want him to try and cut through them even though there's a risk that it could kill your daughter?" he solemnly asked.

Without consulting me, Pete immediately said, "We've got to get rid of this baby, so cut them!"

"Wait a minute," I said, "We've just been told it could kill her."

"This baby will ruin her whole life. It has to be aborted," he shouted.

I tried to change his mind but he was adamant. So, the junior returned to the theatre and the consultant cut the tentacle attached to Cathie's liver. A blue, ink-like substance was released, the tentacle withered and immediately a new one grew to replace it. The operation had failed and she didn't wake up from the anaesthetic. Pete and I were so devastated that we didn't even continue to argue. We went to see Cathie on the ward. She had been given a separate, private room and looked so peaceful.

When the Consultant arrived, he said, "I'm sorry I couldn't do more. She's still alive but in a deep coma. We will probably have to wait until the baby is born before she comes out of it and, hopefully, then she will get better."

Part 2

MY STORY

I will always clearly remember the day when Pete proposed to me. We had spent some time on the beach at Barton-on-Sea and when everyone else had gone home, he went down on one knee, said he loved me and opened a small box, revealing a diamond ring.

"Will you marry me?" he had asked.

He knew that I was part alphan, that our children might be born looking alien and so I would have to give birth to them at home and that I suffered from episodes of depression but none of that had deterred him. Every time we arrived on Alpha, my alphan features returned and this had shocked Pete when I first took him there on my hopper. However, he had become accustomed to the change in me over the following visits and to other alphas calling me Astra, instead of my Earth name, Amanda.

"It's beautiful!" I had exclaimed, trying the ring on. "And it fits perfectly. Have you spoken to my alphan mother and my Earth parents about this?"

"Of course and they are all happy for us, so what do you feel?"

"Yes, yes!" I had exclaimed, bursting into tears of joy, "This is the happiest day of my life."

"Don't cry," he had said, hugging me then passionately kissing me.

Eventually, after a long engagement, we were married at the Silver Sands resort in Barbados. It was a small affair but with a vicar which was important to me. It was so romantic, getting married in glorious sunshine whilst standing on the beach. The wedding planner and the photographer were the only other people there and so they were our witnesses but when we returned home, we had a huge party with family and friends to celebrate properly.

Although Pete was ten years older than me, he had known me all my life as we were paternal cousins. However, when his father had finally left his mother, my father had naturally taken his brother's side and so we had seen little of Pete and his mother for a long time after that. I was in my mid-twenties when we had met again at his father's funeral and had fallen in love almost immediately. We had seen each other a few times afterwards but we both wanted more than a platonic friendship. It was complicated as he was already in an unhappy, long-term relationship. I had visited my brother in Canada for a month, to try to give him space to decide what he really wanted to do. I had made it clear that he couldn't be with both of us at the same time which would have been easier for him. However, as I had not been prepared to have an affair in secret or to hurt the other woman more than was necessary, I insisted that he had had to choose. Two months after my return, he had moved in with me.

We were both short and plump. I had alphan facial features without the translucent skin but with the snub nose and slitty brown eyes. My Earth mother had wondered about these but, fortunately, her husband had some Chinese ancestry in him and, although it was several generations in the past, she had thought it was the reason for my looks. It was these facial features that had enabled Michael Woodman, once the mighty, greedy, power-hungry King of Megalatta, to recognise me one day, whilst I was shopping in Lyndhurst. It was a massive coincidence that we both lived in the New Forest at that time.

Pete was only a little taller than me but he had wavy brown hair, exquisite blue eyes and an infectious smile. As a teenager he'd had a problem with acne but he had a confident, charismatic personality which attracted girls at school and then young women at university. Pretty women coveted our relationship and he had had plenty of choice. On the other hand, I was shy and quiet in nature, preferring to listen rather than being the 'life and soul' of a party like Pete. I lacked confidence in my social skills but felt comfortable with him and so he was the only man that I had ever felt truly passionate with. As Astra, I was shorter but petite and had more confidence but still lacked Pete's sociability and still distrusted strangers. So, Pete had had to get used to the slight change in my personality, as well as the physical change whenever we went to Alpha and I had to keep spare clothes there as my human clothes were too big for me.

Pete had studied Maths and Economics at Nottingham University and I had a Medical degree from Southampton. However, on that day at Barton-on-Sea we agreed that we would wait until I had finished the Nottingham Psychiatric Rotation, passed the Royal College of Psychiatry exams and established myself as a Consultant before we got married. Meanwhile he would give up the struggle to run a Bridge Magazine and concentrate on establishing his career as a self-employed, Consultant Loss Assessor.

Nine months after our honeymoon in Barbados, we were thrilled when our identical twins were born at home. My pregnancy and labour had been overseen by a good friend of mine, Robert Sanderston, who was a Professor in Obstetrics & Gynaecology. He was one of the very few humans who knew of my alphan background. Fortunately, the twins looked like totally normal, human baby girls and we named them Cathie and Rosie, after my favourite aunts. As Pete's work was going reasonably well, I was able to take a break from my work as a Consultant Psychiatrist to look after them, until they went to junior school. After that, I did contract locum work for a few years.

However, by the time the twins were about eight years old, I was disillusioned with the changes in the NHS, Medicine was getting too stressful for me and my locum posts often kept me away from home during the week. Fortunately, Pete worked from home most of the time so he was able to look after the children, taking them to swimming and gymnastics classes. I had started drinking heavily in the evenings and at the weekends, when I was not 'on call'. Pete strongly disapproved of alcohol in excess and my violent mood swings were driving him, my children and my friends away. I had enjoyed riding as a child and we had plenty of land for horses, so he suggested that I should start a riding school. I thought long and hard about this and finally decided that my family and friends were more important than Medicine. So, I quit permanently, took several riding lessons to replenish my skills and opened a riding school for children, becoming abstinent from alcohol shortly afterwards.

The reason why I had alphan as well as human parents was because I had originally been born on and brought up on Alpha Centauri Bb. Having helped to save my race from the evil megalattans, I was poisoned by an alphan witch and traitor, called Mercia. The poison had caused my brain to deteriorate and I had been slowly dying. A relatively new process called Embryolization was used to save me. My DNA was taken from my cells, made invisible and coated with a substance that attracted sperm. My human host mother to be was having IVF treatment and her eggs had already been harvested, waiting for my host father's sperm to fertilise them. The alphan scientist who had developed the Embryolization process had visited Earth himself and had managed to slip my DNA into her eggs. Exactly how this was done, I will never know, as it was kept secret. Fortunately, it worked for me and I was born again on Earth looking like a normal human baby. Sadly, when the alphas had been forced to try it again on a larger scale, a few years later, it had failed. I had been really upset to hear that my two favourite alphan brothers, Onus and Dex, had both died this way, when they had been miscarried at three months.

My human childhood had certainly had its difficulties. Secretly, I resented my Earth mother for favouring my younger brother over me and treating us differently. However, since I had been to university, we had got on much better and she was a wonderful grandmother to my children. The twins had both enjoyed visiting her, especially at weekends or in the school holidays, when we were busy.

The hopper had been made for me by my alphan mother, with the help of her assistant, Dilda, who had some exceptional powers. The hopper consisted of two magic broomsticks, called Fred and George, clamped together with strong metal in three places. There was a post with a magic bangle attached to it which I had to hold onto during re-entry to a planet. It had rubber seats for four people, oxygen tanks with masks and a cooching device (making it able to remain hidden), as well as a lot more electronics. There was a special sheet that could be switched on to cover us to keep us warm when out in space and an intercom system. It could fly through doors and windows and it had some special time-travelling properties which meant it could move much faster than the speed of light. In particular, it only took twenty minutes to get to Alpha and time spent there would not count on Earth. Although, we would be older, we would always arrive back home, about forty minutes after we had left. Fred and George could speak alphanese and powered the hopper by eating Walker's plain crisps.

Alpha was governed by the Supreme Leader. For most of my life that had been my alphan mother, affectionately known as Moma Bara, but she had died just after meeting my twins – it had been almost like she had been hanging on to meet them.

Moma Cara had been the obvious choice to replace her. She had always been a stalwart supporter of my mother but she had briefly left politics when her husband had died suddenly, from a multiple heart attack, leaving her grieving and pregnant with sextuplets. It wasn't that unusual for females on Alpha to have four to six babies in one pregnancy. She had been consumed by grief for the loss of her husband but when she had given birth to her children and was feeling better, she had returned to serve on the High Council. When the General Election was called, after my mother's death, Moma Cara was asked to stand for the post of Supreme Leader and had won with a considerable majority. Unlike the political situation my mother had suffered when I lived on Alpha, Moma Cara's democratically elected parliament listened to her. Consequently, they continued to invest in the technology required to make more effective weapons and build better space battleships to protect Alpha from another invasion.

Many years earlier, Alpha had been virtually defenceless when the mighty Megalon, the King of Megalatta, had invaded to take its stocks of bagaloo, a food that once it had been heated turned into anything that you would like to eat. It grew on the trees on Alpha and could be picked freely by the population as long as they did not hoard more than they needed for a week or when a government harvest was going on to store food for the autumn and winter months. Then the alphas would have to queue at specific distribution points to collect their weekly supplies.

At the age of ten, I had helped to defeat Megalon and he was left for dead on the battlefield. However, while appearing dead, he had used his inner core strength to stay just alive and for a considerable fee, Mercia, the witch who subsequently poisoned me, had revived him. He was now called Michael Woodman and was living on Earth with his favourite wife, Sonja, and their twin boys, David and Paul. They were peacefully settled in Brockenhurst as farmers which was not very far from our home in Lyndhurst. Of course, in order to hide their true identity as megalattans, they all had to have a muscular injection of humanising solution every day.

When they had first been on Earth, Sonja had set up a business in loans. She had not been averse to using force to collect cash from her unfortunate victims who were unwilling or unable to make the heavy repayments.

She had employed her sons as enforcers but, during the last collection that they had tried to make, they had been severely beaten up by their intended victim, called Alan. Coincidently, he happened to lodge with Richard who was an old university friend of mine.

We had met up with Richard and Alan for Sunday lunch at a local pub when the Woodmans had turned up apparently looking to exact revenge on Alan. They had already destroyed Richard's house and they blew up both of our cars. Their anger was not driven so much by Alan's failure to make the loan repayments but rather the condition of their sons. They were so severely compromised by the battering that Alan had given them that they had returned to megalattan type. Both badly needed medical treatment but clearly could not be treated in any hospital on Earth.

When Michael had addressed me as Astra, I had had no doubt as to who we were dealing with. So, I had arranged for all of us to visit Alpha where we could utilise Dilda's skills and magic to revive the two teenagers. After this Sonja had been persuaded to give up her business and the whole family currently lived and worked on the farm.

Dilda was known as 'The Prime Intelligence' and provided telepathic knowledge, healthcare and magic to the Supreme Leader of Alpha. She had helped my mother, Moma Bara, to make my hopper. She was about five feet tall and was half creature and half machine. Her mechanical parts were attached to her abdomen and the wires from the metal box ran up her spinal cord to her brain. She had arms and legs like the rest of us, stood upright and I had been in telepathic contact with her ever since I'd been born on Alpha and then again when I was reborn on Earth. After Mercia had been executed for poisoning me as well as the dragons who had helped to save our planet, Dilda's cave was extended and all Mercia's books and equipment were moved there. As a result, Dilda's knowledge of healing and magic had vastly improved.

We all had thought that the Woodmans were the last megalattans alive as their planet had been nuked by the other planets in their solar system. The others had been tired of the megalattans raiding their food supplies and stealing their precious stones. As a result, Megalatta had imploded into their solar system's sun. Although we were careful not to talk about our alien connections in other people's company, we had become firm friends with Michael and Sonja. The farming had changed them and they had become more peaceful. Both of them would rather walk away from an argument than get embroiled in it. So different from the greedy, power hungry megalattans that they had been. Michael even came to a market auction with me to choose the best ponies for my riding school.

Michael was tall and slim and wore his dark hair tied back in a pony-tail. He had a patch over his right eye, a sad reminder of the bagaloo war on Alpha where, as Astra, I had shot him in that eye. Sonja always looked gorgeous and had not really aged. She had petite facial features and figure, as well as naturally long, blond, wavy hair. I had always envied her looks and her ability to charm any male in our social group. I had often thought that if I started injecting humanising solution, I might end up looking like Sonja. However, I had to dismiss the idea, as Michael had to spend one day a week making enough for his family. His boys, as he liked to call them, were now in their thirties and were also tall with dark brown hair and eyes but much more muscular. They were working on the farm as well and had shown Michael how to use his lap top to do all the necessary IT work, including the accounting.

Meanwhile, Cathie was still in a coma. Rosie had been told this and that she was pregnant with an unusual baby that could not be aborted. Rosie responded by taking Cathie's favourite music into the hospital and sitting with her for hours, while she played the music to try and wake Cathie up but it was useless. In particular, I felt very guilty for putting her life at risk and the relationship with Pete became very frosty for the second time in our marriage.

Then we heard that three other fifteen-year-old girls, who we knew, had gone missing. All of them had complained of being previously 'knocked out', becoming pregnant and having a reptilian rash on their abdomens. One was the daughter of a rich landlord in the village and the other two were in the same year as the twins at school.

The police were baffled. All they knew was that the girls spoke fluent English, were fifteen years old, had all complained of becoming pregnant without their consent and had a reptilian rash. They were all extremely fit and came from mostly affluent backgrounds. The police carried out searches all around the village concentrating, in particular, on the paths the children used to get to school. Some paths and roads around the village were cordoned off and there were police helicopters flying over the woods and the stream that ran through it. They found some of the girls' clothing but none of the girls nor their bodies and, without evidence, they had to call off the search.

The news hit the media by storm which made the police look useless and incompetent. We did tell them the information that Cathie had given us but they had thought that her story was a bit far-fetched. They really wanted to talk to her in private as she fitted into their profile and they thought that she would tell them the truth but of course, this was not possible.

To make matters worse, English-speaking fifteen-year-olds began to go missing from all over the world. There were nearly a thousand of them and their families were distraught. Once they realised that the police had no clues as to where they had gone, they gathered together and a memorial was built in Hyde Park, in London, where they could mourn the loss of their children.

Pete and I hardly spoke in the weeks following Cathie's failed operation. Both of us were shocked by what had happened to her and the desperate state she was in. Both of us were feeling guilty and it was all too easy to want to offload any blame on each other. The situation felt so bad that I thought Pete was going to ask me for a divorce. I had become depressed and had started drinking again, inevitably resulting in mood swings. Pete was spending quite a bit of time away and was taking mobile phone calls all the time, when he was at home. I did not think it significant at the time but he would always go into his office and shut the door before he answered them. Also, some of his clothes and a holdall were missing. Then one day he found a half empty vodka bottle in an upturned, large lampshade in the garage. An argument ensued.

"This is why you've been so moody," he shouted showing me the bottle.

"I'm depressed, I can't cope anymore and you are never around these days and even when you are, you're not talking to me."

"You mean you're not talking to me."

"That's right blame me. It was your decision to have the tentacles cut."

"You didn't exactly stop it happening. I've had enough of you, I'm going to stay with Cassie."

"Whose Cassie?" I inquired, shakily.

"If you must know she's a new friend whose supporting me because you obviously can't."

"What kind of friend? Why haven't we been introduced?"

"Look at the state you're in. It would be too embarrassing."

Now everything began to make sense. The numerous phone calls. The missing clothes.

"You're having an affair, aren't you?" I whispered, hardly daring to ask.

"It's none of your business!" he shouted, walking out and slamming the door.

I collapsed onto the sofa and burst into floods of tears. How could he be doing this to Rosie and me? I had trusted him but now he was heading away into the arms of another woman.

I needed moral support and got in touch with Dilda by telepathy, asking if I could visit Alpha. A few minutes later, Dilda told me that I would be welcome. So, I tidied my hair, wiped away the tears and put on fresh clothing. Then, I got the hopper out of the garage. With all that had been happening, I had forgotten to feed Fred and George. They were starving. Feeling guilty, I opened up a whole box of the crisps. While they were eating, I knocked back the rest of the bottle that Pete had found and grabbed another full one from its hiding place.

It would only take me forty minutes on the hopper to get to Alpha and back and I could spend days there which would not be missed on Earth. As Rosie was out, I closed all the windows and locked all the doors to our house. Then, I got into the driving seat of the hopper, switched it to 'cooch' so we couldn't be seen and flew through the front door, using new oxygen tanks. All it needed from me was to turn off the oxygen and hold the bangle and my breath for thirty seconds while entering Alpha's atmosphere. I landed outside the cave that Dilda lived in just as it was getting dark and realised that I had changed into my alphan form. With long black hair and translucent skin, I fitted in perfectly with the local population.

Moma Cara and Dilda heard my arrival and came out to greet me. Dilda still had the chain around her neck for her own safety as there had been times when she had wandered off and got into trouble. I greeted them both with a hug, grabbed my bottle of vodka and entered Dilda's cave. Without even bothering to change, I got a glass from the cupboard and poured myself a large one. Then knocked it back in one gulp.

"What's happened? You're not drinking again, are you? You know how it affects you!" Dilda frowned.

"Not you as well," I slurred.

"Astra are you drunk?"

"I suppose…."

"What's the matter?"

"Cathie's still in a coma and Pete's having an affair with someone called Cassie."

"Well, drinking is not going to help," she said sternly, taking the bottle away and pouring its contents down the sink.

"What did you do that for? I needed that!"

"Like a house on fire!" she replied. "I think you should get changed then rest. You had better stay here and use the couch. I'll talk to you in the morning when you're sober."

Dilda woke up to find me searching her cave.

"If it's alcohol you're looking for, it's all been chucked away. Now sit down and I'll tell you my plan."

She handed me four pills and a glass of water. I could hardly hold them because of the shaking.

"These are the beginning of your detox regime. They are the alphan equivalent of Librium and will get rid of the tremor."

"I would really rather have another drink!"

"I'm sure you would but you won't be able to sort your life out until you're 'dry' again. You came to me for help and help is what you're going to get. Now, swallow the pills please. Tonight, I will give you the alphan equivalent of mirtazapine, the antidepressant that helped you before."

"Where is Moma Cara?"

"She's left it to me to sort you out. She doesn't drink, as you know, and doesn't really understand why good people destroy their lives with it."

"Ok, so now I've alienated her too,"

"Only temporarily."

I must have stayed on Alpha for almost a month, resting on the sand, swimming in the red sea, watching the dazzling sunsets and spending the evenings talking to Dilda about my problems. She hadn't known about them despite us being connected by telepathy because, as a child, I had learnt to hide things from her. She mainly listened as it all came pouring out but this was useful in itself. Eventually, I felt that I could be in control again and strong enough to return to Earth.

Of course, at home I would have only been away for forty minutes but I would actually be a month older. This worried me a little as I had spent quite a lot of time on Alpha over the years and maybe this would make me look prematurely old on Earth. Then I thought that there was not much sign of ageing as yet and alphas can live for up to two hundred years. Indeed, my alphan mother, Moma Bara, had been one hundred and fifty years old when she had died so perhaps I would have a longer than average life-span for a human.

When I was ready to go, Moma Cara joined us for bagaloo heated on an open fire. My apologies for my behaviour were accepted and she wished me well.

I thanked Dilda profusely and left the following morning before anyone was awake.

When I got back home, Rosie had just returned from the hospital.

"Hi, mum," she said. "No change with Cathie, I'm afraid. Have you seen Dad?"

"Rosie, we had a massive row and he left to stay with a friend. I'm sorry, but I don't know when he'll be back."

For the next few months we settled into something of a routine. I would visit Cathie during the day when Rosie was at school, Rosie would normally visit in the evenings and at weekends. Rosie was besotted with Michael's son, Paul, so the only variations were when she visited the Woodmans to see him or when I went to see Michael and Sonja.

After eight months of her pregnancy, Cathie developed pre-eclampsia, a very high blood pressure and protein in her urine. An abdominal CT scan revealed that the tentacles, which the foetus had previously extended into Cathie's organs, had withered away so Cathie's baby was delivered by Caesarean Section.

My friend Professor Robert Sanderston, who was now retired, had offered to adopt the child and was there with me at the birth. Out came this alien baby which the midwife and others witnessed. Sanderston took a photo of it straight away. The baby looked very much like the description of his father but obviously smaller.

Within five minutes, he had turned into a normal looking human child and, after the easy delivery of the placenta, was handed over to the Professor. After a quick check, he took him away, saying that he would call him Mark.

Sanderston asked everyone there to keep quiet about the alien nature of the child but the midwife said she would have to tell the Consultant who had operated on Cathie. Somehow the press had heard the news and were waiting to see Mark. When Sanderston showed them a normal looking human baby, they were disappointed and so lost interest in the story.

Two weeks later another fifteen-year-old was admitted in labour. Her story was very similar to Cathie's and another alien was born but female this time. The Consultant and Sanderston insisted that photos be taken, as soon as possible, after the baby was born and Sanderston eventually adopted this child too, naming her Julia. Now he had both male and female alien children. Everyone thought that he was just a middle-aged philanthropist. No-one thought that he wanted these children to experiment on them!

The Consultant who had operated on Cathie had already written to the British Medical Journal, the BMJ, to warn other surgeons not to try to abort these babies if the mother had a reptilian rash on her abdomen and there were tentacles reaching into her vital organs. These could now be observed on a CT scan. Julia's mother had had this as she had also wanted an abortion. There had been some news coverage at the time but the photos of the baby straight after birth had been hidden away in a safe vault. Most people and the press thought that they were just human mutants and not dangerous.

Meanwhile, Cathie was still in a coma but at least the rash on her abdomen had started to fade. It was a Saturday, about two weeks later, when I got home with the shopping and Rosie rushed in.

"Cathie's awake, the rash has gone completely and she is asking for you and Dad. Do you know how to contact him?"

"Let's go and see Cathie first."

Cathie was so pleased to see us but wondered where her dad was. I explained that he had gone away for a while but would be back soon. She had already been told that she had been in a coma for nearly six months and that her baby had been adopted. She was upset having looked at the scars but I tried to console her by saying that they would fade with time.

Then I asked if she felt well enough to talk to the police, as they were waiting outside. She agreed and they entered the room. Cathie told the police the same story but, of course, they didn't believe her. When she went back to school, it was a little difficult and embarrassing at first, as she was put in the year below Rosie but she soon made new friends.

Then one day, she came home early, having told her teacher that she was feeling unwell. She seemed distressed and distracted so I asked her to explain.

"Mum, you have to keep it secret!"

"Well, it depends on what the problem is and whether you need to see your GP?"

"Mum, I'm seeing things and hearing voices in flashes."

"Ok," I said, concerned. "I have to ask you a few simple questions but you must promise to answer me truthfully."

She nodded.

"Firstly, are the voices inside your head or outside your head?" I asked, trying to ascertain whether she was hearing second or third person voices.

"No, they're inside."

"Ok, is it your own voice, your thoughts being heard out loud?" I asked, thinking of thought echo.

"No."

"And the pictures, what are they of?"

"Creatures like the one who raped me, talking in a language I can't understand."

"Well, you're not becoming psychotic or going mad, if that's what you thought."

"Thank God for that!" she exclaimed, somewhat relieved.

Then, to ascertain whether she was having flashbacks, I asked more about the pictures.

"There's a creature, just like the one who raped me, shouting at a group of slightly smaller and less muscular creatures who look frightened of him and call him Zygon."

"Cathie this reminds me so much of my telepathic contact with Dilda. I think that you are in the same kind of contact with this alien called Zygon. Now, listen very carefully to me, telepathy works both ways. You have to keep it hidden from Zygon, otherwise your life could be in danger again. Do you think you can do this?"

"Mum, I will try,"

"And try not to focus on these 'flashes' if you're concentrating on your studies. It might be helpful if Michael could teach you Megalonese, then you would be able to understand them. Cathie, this is a gift. Learn to use it correctly, as it could prove useful to us but for the time being only Michael and I will know."

"Thank you, Mum. I really thought I was going mad."

"I know, so did I at first."

"I'll tell the head teacher that you're being troubled by memories of your rape and that if this continues, we'll get you some counselling. You're right, we do have to keep this secret."

The only problem that remained was Pete. It had been four months since the row and it was only after this time that I felt like dealing with another confrontation. So, one evening, when the girls were out, I phoned his mobile.

"Hi, how are you?"

"Cassie and I have split up but I have been feeling too guilty to come home."

"The girls have been trying to call you,"

"I know but I didn't know what you'd told them or whether you wanted me back?"

"I said we'd had a row and that you'd gone to live with a friend,"

"That was good of you. Much appreciated."

"I'm dry now," I said. "Dilda helped me. Cathie's back at school and both of the children are really missing you. I am too."

"That's great news! I'm sorry I cheated on you. I should have stayed and helped you but I didn't know how. Can you forgive me?"

"Of course, darling. I phoned you, didn't I? How far away are you?"

"About an hour's drive."

"Ok! Come home now and I'll have some supper waiting for you."

Part 3

SONJA'S STORY

I will always remember the day that Michael contacted me because of his concern for his wife's health. Cathie was still unconscious in hospital, at the time, and Michael started by saying how sorry he was to have heard about what had happened to her – Rosie had told them all about it on one of her trips to visit Michael's son, Paul. However, at least to my mind, Sonja's story was even more horrific. Michael told me what had happened.

An alien but recognisable spacecraft had landed on his farm. It was large and took up most of the one-acre field, it had a relatively small cockpit and was obviously used for carrying people as it had windows along each side of its hold. Although its shields had been down, they were clearly visible and except for the faint humming of engines, it had appeared to come out of nowhere, as it had been cooched. Sonja had been in one of the fields nearby and two beefy megalattans had got out and abducted her. Once on board the ship, she had been raped and held hostage. Michael's camper van had also been raided and the book of spells that Mercia had given him, had sprouted legs and tried to walk off. Although it had been restrained by its chain, it had obviously been disturbed but not taken.

It transpired that the megalattans on board the spacecraft had managed to escape from their planet, just before it was completely destroyed but the nuclear fallout had rendered their females infertile. Their leader, Zygon, had been so annoyed by this that he had ejected their females into space - possibly a mistake as his crew had been starved of any female company. They had all been particularly taken by Sonja, once the humanising solution had worn off. This was not just because she was the first megalattan woman they had seen in years but also because she had lime green skin and an attractive row of reptilian points running across her head. Every male on board the craft had wanted to have sex with her. Zygon, himself, had been the first to rape her.

The ransom that they had demanded from Michael was a supply of humanising solution and the method to make some more. Although, Zygon's scientists had already made a vaccine to make alien babies look human a few minutes after birth, they had been struggling to find a way of actually making themselves look human. Michael had not known what to do. He'd realised that some of the megalattans must have got away before their planet had imploded into its sun but he had no idea that they were going to use human teenagers to be hosts for a new race of hybrids.

Zygon had come to talk to Michael himself. He'd escaped with a number of scientists, ministers of state and some bully boys who were larger, fearsome creatures as well as some of their wives. The nuclear fallout had had a very different effect on the adult men who had mutated and now fed on the negative emotions of others. While ejecting their females into space had left his crew sexually frustrated, it had had the positive effect of keeping his followers fed because of their females' distress. They had searched for a new planet to settle on for some years and, in the respect of keeping his crew well-fed, the human race was certainly good fodder. There were so many natural disasters for the zygonites to enjoy and they had indulged themselves, whilst following wars all over the world along with the details of how badly some governments treated their own people. In the event of a drought of bad news, it was not difficult for Zygon to stir up trouble himself. He could cause 'natural' disasters and had very well-developed telepathic powers. Of course, it had been those powers that had drawn his attention to the fact that there was a family of megalattans on Earth who appeared to have taken human form.

Zygon had made it perfectly clear that if Michael hadn't helped them, they would have tortured and disposed of Sonja and, no doubt, they would have tortured and killed Michael and both of his sons. Michael had dreaded to think what would happen to the human race but had been so worried about his wife that he'd given them what they had wanted. Sonja had been returned to him, naked and pregnant with another creature's child and the zygonites had left.

The boys had been horrified to see their mother in her natural megalattan form.

Paul had asked his father, "Is that what we look like without the humanising solution?"

"Of course," he had answered, "But not so beautiful."

He had immediately given Sonja a humanising injection. She was bruised all over and bleeding heavily from her vagina where she had been brutalised. At first, she flinched from his touch but then she had fainted so at least he had been able to transport her upstairs. Michael had got her dressed in her pyjamas and put her to bed. Then he had called me.

When I arrived, the bed and her clothing were soaked in green blood. I pleaded with Michael to let me take her to Alpha for Dilda's help. Just like her sons had done when they had been severely beaten, she had returned to her alien form, despite the humanising injection. I knew she would die without treatment but we couldn't take her to any ordinary hospital on Earth.

Eventually, MIchael agreed. He knew that Paul and David's blood types were the same as hers and they came with us to donate much needed blood for a transfusion. With a simple alphan spell that Mercia had given him, Michael could turn his camper van into a space buggy. So, we travelled to Alpha in it, as Sonja couldn't sit up. The space buggy was cramped but had seats that could be made into beds, outside shields and a small cockpit. It could also time travel and be cooched. Dilda was outside ready to greet us and immediately transported Sonja to an operating table.

After thirty minutes of stitching and several blood transfusions, her vital signs returned to normal and she was physically on the mend but mentally still traumatised and would be for some time to come. Once Sonja had come around from the anaesthetic, Dilda gave her an injection of humanising solution and organised for an excellent alphan counsellor to come and talk to her. Alphas were friendly towards humans, mainly because of me and my hybrid nature so Sonja was not in any danger in human form. The counsellor seemed to help her but she didn't want anything to do with us and when we approached her, she just flew into a rage. Dilda recognised that it was going to take some considerable time for Sonja to recover. So, she kindly suggested that Sonja could stay with her for as long as necessary and started giving her daily alphanising injections which had already become available on Alpha. Dilda said that she would keep us informed of what progress was being made.

There was nothing else for us to do so Michael, his sons and I returned home to Earth. Over the next couple of months, despite his reservations about her alphan form, Michael visited her regularly but Sonja wouldn't let him touch her, not even for a friendly, comforting hug. He was furious and would gladly have assassinated Zygon himself, when and if given the opportunity.

Eventually, it became clear to everybody that Sonja was both confused and mentally unwell. She kept on refusing to have her daily alphanising injections which were necessary because in megalattan form she would have the ability to transport herself out of Dilda's cave. Alphas and megalattans were old enemies so she would be in danger, if she wandered around Alpha in her native form.

It was Cathie who came up with a possible solution. By then, she had recovered from her ordeal and was back at school. As a host mother of one of the hybrid babies she had found that she was in telepathic contact with the Zygon elite. She was highly intelligent and, with tutoring from Michael, she had managed to understand technological as well as conversational Megalonese. It had some similarities to Latin which she had learnt at school. As she had suspected, the technological elements quickly proved to be useful.

Listening into their conversations, she had discovered that Zygon's scientists had been able to make a depot of the humanising solution which they thought would last for at least six months. Although Cathie didn't understand all that she had heard, she was able to garner sufficient information to explain enough of the process to Dilda. This was done via telepathy, as her newly-found powers extended to Dilda, as well as the zygonites. So, Dilda was able to replicate the long-acting, depot of humanising solution. This depot solution was of great assistance to all the Woodmans except Sonja who needed to look and be alphan for the time being, as she could transport herself out of the cave in human but not in alphan form. However, Dilda was able to adapt the methodology to create an alphanising depot so it was just a case of pinning Sonja down to give it to her. This was not so easy. In the end, Dilda had to lace her tea with a strong sedative before administering the long-acting, alphanising depot.

Soon afterwards, Dilda suggested that I should visit to observe Sonja and advise what psychiatric medication might be of assistance to her. It was easy for me to diagnose Sonja as having mania. She was not sleeping or eating at all. She was convinced that if she slept she would die and wouldn't eat as she explained that food was talking directly to her in the second person and was alive and therefore not edible. She was also hearing 'third person voices', outside her head, which were mainly her dead family arguing about her. She would have conversations with these voices as no-one could persuade her that they were not real. She was also speaking so rapidly and with a lot of puns and rhyming slang that it was often difficult to understand her. Even though she was fluent in Alphanese, she would swop languages in mid-flow and she wouldn't sit still. Instead, she paced or danced around Dilda's cave until exhaustion got the better of her. Then, there were times when the acceleration of her thoughts made the associations in her speech so loose and the goal so elusive that it was unintelligible.

"Now she's talking nonsense!" Dilda complained.

"I think it might be what's known as 'flight of ideas,'" I replied.

"Well, you would know. What are we going to do? She never sleeps and, although she gets irritable and aggressive about it, someone has to prevent her from leaving the cave. I think, even in alphan form, she would be in grave danger outside and probably wouldn't be able to find her way back."

"Thankfully she can't transport herself at the moment but I know she needs continual care and we are both exhausted. I think she needs professional help in hospital. We've tried offering her the appropriate tablets, or the alphan equivalents, but she has no insight and says she doesn't need them. I'm sure that she would improve with an antipsychotic by depot injection. Let's try to persuade her to go into hospital."

We both did our best but the lack of insight won. In a lucid moment she said that she felt incredibly good, in fact better than she'd ever been and obviously didn't want medication to take the 'high' away. Much to our regret, she had to be sectioned and then admitted to a private psychiatric hospital, on Alpha. Michael tried to visit her there but she only went into a fit of temper and hit him. She was too tiny to hurt him but the message was clear and he was asked to wait until she was better before visiting again.

When I visited her, it was different as she would talk to me. In a lucid moment she was able to tell me that, since their leader was called Zygon and his race had mutated, his people referred to themselves as 'zygonites'. Sonja would rant and rave about them but I was able to ascertain that she was unsure why her family were arguing about her. She was puzzled by the meaning of the voices but she thought that her closest family and friends were plotting to kill her because they were jealous. No amount of reassurance from me seemed to help and for a time she wouldn't meet with me at all.

At night, she couldn't sleep and would run up and down the corridors of the hospital, banging on peoples' doors and waking them up. She had to be secluded, locked up in a private room, and pinned down to be given a sedative, on several occasions. Initially, this seemed to work and, afterwards, she would be quieter for a few days.

I approached Michael and asked if he would help me with the Megalonese language. I had learnt it at school on Alpha but was somewhat rusty with it by then. I thought that if I talked to Sonja in her native tongue, I might make more sense of her conversation. However, she was speaking so quickly and using a lot of rhyming slang that, even in her mother-tongue, her speech was hard to follow. Most of the time she just spoke gibberish but there would be the odd occasions when she would become lucid and then she would say that she felt great and wanted to come home. Her favourite 'party piece' was to get up and swirl around in circles until she fell over, saying in English,

"Look I can still dance so give me a chance and take me home."

However, they could not keep on sedating her as her tiny body would not be able to take it and the process was traumatic for her. There were dark rings under her eyes from lack of sleep and she had become incredibly thin. There was talk of force-feeding her but this would have only added to the emotional trauma. Exasperated that she had not been given an anti-psychotic depot, I went to see the Chief of Psychiatry at the hospital and introduced myself.

"I was a Consultant Psychiatrist before," I said. "I feel that Sonja would become better with the antipsychotic olanzapine which I believe you can give in depot form?"

"Why an olanzapine depot?" he asked.

"Olanzapine would help to stabilise her mood and increase her appetite, as well as helping with the delusions and auditory hallucinations and I don't think she would take tablets or tolerate blood tests, so lithium is out of the question."

Lithium is a mood stabiliser which is commonly used to treat mania but has a small therapeutic range. Too little renders it useless and too much is toxic. Blood tests have to be done regularly to ascertain a lithium level and alter the dose accordingly. Furthermore, I didn't know what would be the appropriate dosage of lithium for a megalattan, albeit one disguised as an alpha.

"Well Dr. Phillips," he said to me, "I'm willing to give it a try."

They had to pin her down again to administer the depot but, after only two weeks on just the olanzapine, she was calmer and Michael was able to visit her again. He was so pleased that when he saw her she was pleasant and gave him a hug. He was not too sure about the obvious muscle-wasting in her arms and legs and the dark shadows under her eyes but he was glad that she was on the mend and was eating again.

Then overnight she became depressed, would not stop crying, stopped eating again and was expressing suicidal thoughts and even plans. She became paranoid, complaining that her thoughts were running down her body from her head and being broadcast to everyone around her. I went to the head of the hospital again,

"She needs an antidepressant as well," I said.

"But won't that bring back her mania?"

"Not if you increase the dose of the olanzapine depot and use a depot of mirtazepine that I think is available on Alpha. The mirtazapine will also help her sleep. We've got to do something! The depression following mania is one of the worst kinds and would be unrelenting, until she eventually finds a way to kill herself."

"I see," he said. "Okay, Dr. Phillips, you know her better than I do and your previous suggestion helped so I'm willing to give it a try but you will have to take responsibility, if it all goes terribly wrong."

"I'm willing to do that," I said "Thank you, sir."

It took three months for her to come around to her usual sunny, pleasant disposition and with intensive daily counselling, she had improved sufficiently to have a trial of home leave. Dilda and Moma Cara welcomed her with open arms and she was able to sit and talk rationally about what had happened to her. She knew that she had a schizoaffective disorder, the formal name for a type of manic depression mixed with schizophrenia and would be on the medication for the rest of her life.

A friend of mine, a practising Psychiatric Consultant, on Earth was happy to take on her case and prescribe the medication in tablet form but I had to discuss it with Michael first, as I needed to reveal her true identity, as a megalattan. Michael was, naturally, apprehensive but, eventually, agreed that I could say that she was a friendly alien who worked peacefully on a farm and used a humanising depot. When I told my friend, he was curious but I explained that her home planet had been destroyed by nuclear war. He was sympathetic and agreed to take on Sonja, as a patient. So, once the Chief of Psychiatry on Alpha realised he could hand over the case to a Consultant on Earth, he discharged her. Dilda allowed the alphanising depot to wear off, before giving her a humanising one and Michael came to pick her up. He had worried about her pregnancy and how he would bring up another creature's child but, during her manic phase, she had had a miscarriage, which was a relief for all concerned.

Part 4

THE ALIENS' STORY

Sonja Woodman will always remember the day when we thought that she was ready to hear about what had happened to Cathie. Sonja had been back on Earth for about a week, when we all went over to visit the Woodmans. Sonja had already been examined by my friend, her Consultant Psychiatrist, and she was doing well. Despite what had happened to her she was shocked and clearly empathic towards Cathie. Sonja felt that Cathie's experience must have been worse than her own because at least she had been raped by her own kind.

We made certain to assure both Michael and Sonja that what had happened to Cathie was clearly not their fault. Cathie had been impregnated a considerable time before the zygonites had had humanising solution. Furthermore, while the humanising solution would make it much easier for the zygonites to conceal themselves on Earth, their plan to make human girls

54

bear hybrid offspring had been well-advanced before Michael had been forced to give them the solution.

Michael was clearly embarrassed by the fact that his own race, albeit now mutated, had stooped to such a low level and, of course, he was still furious about what they had done to Sonja. He expressed his determination to kill Zygon again and to destroy what had once been his own people.

About this time, an astronomer called Davidson had been using an infra-red light telescope and had discovered a second but much smaller moon orbiting the Earth, partially hidden behind the real moon. He had noticed what he thought were spacecraft piercing its surface to enter or exit it, although he couldn't see these ships, as they were cooched. The idea that this is where the missing teenagers had gone and that there were aliens on Earth was, initially, dismissed as preposterous. However, Cathie was able to confirm his story via her telepathic connection with the Zygon elite: human teenagers were definitely incarcerated on the Mother Ship he'd seen.

We found out later that they were imprisoned like animals and living in terrible, rotten conditions. They were being fed disgusting food that would help their babies grow tentacles. Initially, they were all kept in the hold of the ship with limited light and buckets for toilets. The food caused diarrhoea and the stench was appalling but, as I observed earlier, the aliens didn't have a very good sense of smell. The ones that survived these conditions were taken up to a birthing area when they went into labour. No pain relief was provided and the babies were taken away from their mothers, as soon as they were born. They were put in a creche and looked after by zygonite guards.

The women would then be taken back down to the hold area and the aliens would leave them alone for a month before impregnating them again. Talk about 'highly respected', there was no respect at all; they were just hybrid-making machines. They didn't even have proper beds to lie on, only plastic mats! The humans that had had more than one miscarriage or had lost their wombs in childbirth were ejected into space, dead or alive. Of course, this provided good sustenance for the zygonites on board, while leaving the other girls in terror for their lives.

The aliens learnt that trying to impregnate the girls with too many guards made them go into shock and they often died. In some cases, just appearing in their alien form had the same effect but knocking them out, as the alien had done with Cathie, only led to epileptic fits and more miscarriages. So, the zygonites had all been given a humanising depot and every girl was paired with just one alien guard, although the guard could have more than one human partner. There was pressure on the guards too, as many were disposed of if they didn't cause a pregnancy within six months.

The only way to escape the awful conditions of the hold was to pretend to be in love with an impregnator. Then, if he agreed, they would be seen as a couplet and would go through a coupling ceremony, a bit like marriage. Then, the girl would be kept alone, in the guard's room which at least gave her a bed and access to proper bathroom facilities but she would still be aware that her guard had many other human females to impregnate.

In general, the guards were short-tempered and any attempts by the girls to escape led to fractures and bruises all over their bodies which were never dealt with properly. At first, the guards asked if the couplets, could keep their own babies and this worked for a while, until they grew to the age of about two years old. Then, the human mothers just couldn't control them. The hybrids grew up very quickly and at the age of two, they looked more like human six-year olds. A guard would often come back to his room to find it in a complete mess and his female battered and bruised, lying on the floor unconscious. When Zygon found out, his first reaction was to laugh but it was clear that the children had to be taken away. The guards protested but Zygon was adamant. Later, the couplet mothers were allowed to visit their children in the creche, under supervision of zygonite guards, when the children were much better behaved.

Anna was one of the more intelligent human occupants of the Mother Ship's hold. She soon worked out that her living conditions would improve if she appeared to have fallen in love with her impregnator. The guard was quite besotted with her so they had gone through a 'coupling ceremony'. As a result, she had been able to stay in his quarters but, obviously, she was still imprisoned. Soon after giving birth to a hybrid, it was taken away, which upset her partner sufficiently for her to persuade him to hide her on a freighter bound for Earth. He would follow, as soon as he could, so that they could raise their next baby together in a flat that he had been given in England – the home he had used before abducting her.

Unfortunately, the cargo ship landed in Colombia where Zygon had established a thriving base, having taken control of a significant portion of the cocaine trade. Without a passport, Anna had found it difficult to get back to England but she had managed to find her way to a police station and told them all about her capture and the conditions she had been living in. At first, she wasn't believed but the news hit the papers. I was so glad that my Cathie had had the courage to escape the fate of the teenagers on board the Mother Ship. Davidson's theory had been published in the papers world-wide by then and people began to believe in it.

Eventually, Anna got back to England and found her alien partner's flat. She waited there for him for a month but, finally, picked up a telepathic message from Zygon which was so strong that it could not have been mistaken. He was furious and had killed her couplet who he knew had helped her to escape. Distraught and pregnant with his baby, she had travelled back to her family. She came with more news of what had been happening on the Mother Ship and this led to a campaign to destroy it, as soon as possible. Clearly, the teenagers were living lives worse than death and if nothing was done, more girls would be taken.

However, simultaneously, there was also mounting opposition to the idea of using force against the Mother Ship, from the families who had lost their children and had come to believe they were on it. What could the human race do? They didn't have ships that could fly through space and time so there was no logical way they could rescue the teenagers. All they might be able to do was target the aliens' moon with rockets, armed with nuclear warheads. At least, that might destroy the Mother Ship and stop more children being abducted.

The police wanted to interview Cathie again because so many girls had gone missing from all over the world by then and the newspapers were reporting more sightings of the artificial moon.

"I've told them everything I know and don't want to go through the whole sordid story again. I would rather forget it. I just want to be left alone to get on with my life," she complained.

"Well, I'll be with you and think that you will be helping all those girls on the Mother Ship," I replied.

The police had a copy of the photo of Julia, taken just after birth and showed it to her. She responded with a long silence, in which they pressured her. Eventually, she told them her whole story, as she had remembered it, all over again and confirmed that the monster who had raped her looked like the photo only that he was obviously bigger and male. They were particularly interested in the 'safe place' she was going to be taken to but all she knew was that it needed a spacecraft to get there and that she had been told that other teenagers would be there.

Professor Sanderston, or Bob to his friends, and his wife, Beth, were having great trouble raising their adopted children. They could disappear at will and move small objects, then larger ones without touching them. They didn't respond to scolding and if either parent got angry with them, the children would lift them up off the ground and throw them against the wall. Beth and Bob had already sustained several fractures due to this behaviour and all they could do to stop it continuing was to play dead themselves.

Bob had read 'Davidson's report' and went to see him. Using Davidson's infra-red telescope, he could see the second moon for himself. So, he bought an infra-red scanner and found that using it, he could see the children when they vanished. They seemed weaker and more manageable after he'd used the scanner on them. So, he went and bought some powerful infra-red lamps which he thought he might be able to use to control the hybrid children in the future.

One day a strong wind blew over the climbing frame in the garden, while the kids were using it. They had both fallen off and knocked themselves out on the paving stones below. Rather surprisingly, while they were unconscious they had returned to their alien form. Bob took pictures of them lying underneath the frame and then waited for them to recover, as he could not take them to hospital, at least not in their current form.

As the kids came around, their human appearance reappeared. Both of them were really annoyed that the climbing frame had not been more securely attached to the ground. Once again, Bob and Beth had to endure being picked up and thrown around. Later, when the kids were both asleep, Bob set up the infra-red lamps and flooded their bedroom with infra-red light. His initial thought was that this would just weaken the children and make them more manageable but by the morning, they were both dead. Bob and Beth had had more than enough of them, so, whilst not exactly planned, this eventuality was not unwelcome.

Bob's main concern was that he and his wife might be accused of murdering the children so he removed the lights and destroyed them. Then he called the Special Police Squad who had dealt with Cathie's case. They came straight away and Bob explained how the children had died as the result of an accident when they insisted on using the climbing frame, during a gale. Of course, he had pictures to prove it. Certainly, the police had no idea that the hybrids would revert to alien form when they were knocked unconscious – so it did look like they had died as a result of the accident.

The police simply enquired as to why Bob had not left the bodies outside under the climbing frame until they had arrived. Bob explained that he hadn't wanted the bodies to remain in situ just in case they were seen by other people who might have been shocked and, of course, they had not wanted to spark further publicity in the media.

A month later Bob and Beth were both diagnosed with inoperable, metastatic brain tumours and given just a few months to live. They thought that these had been caused by Mark and Julia and the increasing domination of the world by aliens. So, together, they decided to write an article for the BMJ, about bringing up alien children. They outlined what the children had been capable of, how they grew up so quickly at a rate of about three hybrid years in an Earth year and how they had not died from hitting their heads on concrete but through being flooded with infra-red light. They also sent in the pictures of their children in both human and alien form. By this time, although they were only at the age of two Earth years, they looked more like human six-year olds and had had to be tutored at home because of the obvious difference in growth rates.

The BMJ did not know whether to publish the report or not so consulted the police and the government. In closed meetings, away from the press, some ministers spoke out and said the public had a right to know. However, these ministers died very quickly of a fever that no-one could find the cause of or a cure for. Because the government feared that if the report was published it was likely to lead to widespread panic, the consensus was that it should be shelved and the BMJ were instructed not to publish it. However, behind the scenes copies of the report, marked Top Secret, were routinely passed to NATO, France and the USA.

One of these copies landed on the desk of a Colonel Turner in a small office at the Pentagon. His job was to research new ways in which enemies of the United States might find to attack them and prepare defences against them. Back in the 1980's his small department had been instrumental in suggesting the so-called Strategic Defence Initiative to President Reagan. More recently, they had been heavily involved in developing the rather less ambitious Nuclear Missile Defence System that was designed to protect the USA mainland from a limited, nuclear missile attack.

The idea that the Earth might be invaded by aliens, at some stage, was not new to him. Over the years, he had been sent all sorts of zany reports – supposed sightings of flying saucers being not that uncommon. However, there was something about Bob and Beth Sanderston's report that rang true. The report provided detailed observation of alien children who had clearly developed extremely quickly and had capabilities well beyond the scope of normal humans.

The Colonel started by scouring the American press to find any reports of teenage girls being abducted. He was quite shocked when he found out just how many American teenage girls had disappeared in the previous two years. The only good news was that the report had also indicated a potential weakness of the aliens. To a man who was well versed in the actual practicalities of 'Star Wars', it seemed quite feasible that some of the more sophisticated armoury of the United States might be adapted to cope with such aliens. That is, if they actually existed. The USA already had some space laser satellites and their 'spy in the sky' surveillance system already relied on infra-red technology. Without more ado, he authorised defence department scientists to design a satellite system that could target specific locations on Earth and hit them with a concentrated beam of infra-red light. About half of the heat from the sun comes in the form of infra-red light so, in reality, the task was merely a question of concentrating some of the sun's power and sending it in the designated direction.

At governmental level, everyone who knew about the Sanderston report was afraid that the Earth was being colonised by aliens. They had become paranoid that the aliens were intercepting their every move, trying to ensure that their secret plan was not discovered.

In fact, this was exactly what was actually happening. Even the police who had seen the pictures were dying of unknown causes. Some of these deaths had been reported as a virus which was affecting the population, but we knew it was due to the alien's leader, Zygon. He had amazing powers of telepathy and was also able to kill off anyone that posed a threat to his plans of creating a hybrid race which would, eventually, take over Earth. He could even create 'natural' disasters so that both the zygonites and the adult hybrids could feed off the distress of the humans involved. However, his powers were not all-encompassing; yes, he could focus on those who expressed what he thought were dangerous views in government meetings or on the authors of negative reports such as the Sanderstons. The negative vibes of such humans resonated in his mind, making it easy for him to track them down or at least return the vibes with interest!

I frequently wondered why he did not target his retribution on either Michael's family or my own or even on scientists like Davidson. Eventually, it occurred to me that it was many people's revulsion at the appearance of the zygonites and their fear of what the aliens might do that attracted Zygon's attention, rather like a radio beacon. As a part alien myself, I was quite accustomed to what megalattans looked like which had not changed when they had mutated into zygonites and how badly they could behave. Of course, Michael's family, Pete and now Cathie knew all about them too. Meanwhile, Davidson had just reported what he had observed on an entirely unemotional scientific basis. Although Zygon knew he had written a report, he was thwarted by being unable to discover the whereabouts of the author. In a similar way, Colonel Turner approached his job in a scientific manner – he analysed any threat and tried to counter it in an entirely unemotional, objective manner. Consequently, Zygon was totally unaware of Turner's activities.

Then things started to get political! The people of the Western World where most of the abductions had occurred began to blame Russia and the East for taking their children and accused them of conducting biological warfare. There was a growing feeling that World War Three might be 'on the cards'.

Zygon and his team had obviously been keeping a close eye on all of his kind and had been protecting them. While his people thrived on the bad news that was so prevalent on Earth, the last thing he really wanted was an all-out nuclear war which would make the planet uninhabitable. He decided to scale back on the rate he was abducting human girls and try and maintain a relatively low profile for a while. Hopefully, a period of inactivity, on his part, would help to reduce the animosity between the most powerful nations on Earth. Meanwhile, the hybrid children would grow up and his baby factory in space would be able to continue its work. Using his exceptional telepathic powers, he instructed his people on Earth to maintain a low profile and not to use any of their special powers, unless they were caught in death-threatening situations. When he was ready to enact the next stage of his plan, he should be in a much stronger position.

His operation on Earth had become a lot easier since he had acquired the formula for humanising solution from Michael and his scientists had developed a depot form which could last for up to six months. By the time he had been on Earth for five years, he had become a self-made billionaire, mainly as a result of distributing cocaine from Colombia all over the USA. In his human form as Fred Barker, Zygon was an imposing figure. He was six feet four inches tall and weighed over twenty stone. The police knew he was dealing in cocaine but his telepathic powers ensured that he always had advanced warning of when and where they were going to make a raid. He was always able to move his stocks and then vanish. Many of his employees were already in prison but there were plenty more people who he could employ who wanted to work for him, as the pay was very good. However, if anyone went against him, he would use his powers to destroy them and their families. Everyone who knew him was terrified of him.

He had several army-type helicopters which were useful for delivering cocaine supplies and a few planes, as well as a fleet of jeeps. Some people noticed that he never seemed to age and was still able to run his business at the age of eighty.

After his message had been sent, the hybrid children on Earth settled down and became 'normal' teenagers. Over the next couple of years much of the hysteria on Earth dissipated – the decline in the rate of inexplicable abductions and reported alien births combined to foster a false sense of security in most human politicians. Of course, Zygon had dealt with a large proportion of the people who had actually witnessed the alien births and while there were still occasional reports of the second moon in the sky, it seemed to be benign, so coverage in the media rapidly declined.

As hybrid production on his moon spaceship continued, it soon became clear that there was not enough room to accommodate them all sensibly on his Mother Ship and the older hybrids were becoming frustrated by the limited facilities. Zygon responded to this by purchasing an extensive ten-acre plot in South East London which was largely derelict. Then, he successfully obtained planning permission to bulldoze the old disused warehouses on the site, in order to build an estate of flats on the land, along with the other necessary amenities. Of course, Zygon had sweetened the deal by promising that at least half of the estate would be let out at modest rents or sold at prices that the average Londoner could afford. He had also undertaken to finance a long-awaited upgrade of some of the roads in the area.

Most Londoners thought that this was a good step forward as London was desperately short of affordable housing. In reality, the development didn't ease the pressure on housing much. Zygonite hybrids grew up very quickly and the ones who had stayed on Earth, soon became old enough to form relationships within their peer group and live independently of their human parents. So, the only Londoners who were accommodated on the site were actually hybrid teenagers who happened to have been brought up in London. Zygon gathered together a number of hybrids from all over the UK, and quite a selection from the rest of the world, interspersed with hybrids from his moon spaceship to live on his new estate. Single male hybrids were encouraged to choose a female partner: those from Earth had to choose a partner from the Mother Ship and vice versa, those from the moon spaceship had to choose a partner from Earth.

However, something in their genes had mutated and most of the hybrid females still could not get pregnant. The problem was explained to Zygon by one of his scientists who had been studying the physiology of the hybrids that appeared to be adults. Although they had grown up extremely quickly into adult form, their reproductive organs had not kept pace with the rest of their development. Basically, they looked old enough to have babies of their own but the females were too young to get pregnant. So, for the time-being, Zygon issued them with hybrid babies from his moon ship to look after and paid them well for the task of bringing them up. All of them that were old enough wanted a baby or two to look after to obviate the need to take the trouble of getting a regular job.

Clearly, Zygon knew that there was a substantial risk that the host mothers might become telepathic having carried an alien baby, just like Cathie had done. He, therefore, had instructed the Earth-based hybrids to kill their mothers before moving to his estate in South-East London. As far as possible, this should be done to look like they had either died in accidents or from natural causes. However, some of the children didn't know they'd been adopted so they didn't kill their real mothers and some of the hybrids just couldn't bring themselves emotionally to kill their mothers who had looked after them since birth. They did their best to keep this hidden from Zygon.

In the end, there were about fifty host mothers who had survived the cull on Earth and all of them had developed some telepathic powers. Most of them had some contact with their alien offspring and with each other.

The mass killings provoked the police again as none of the humans affected showed any kind of damage with guns or knives. In the main, their hearts had just stopped beating. The BMA, the British Medical Association, in conjunction with the British and American Governments decided to release Sanderston's report with the photos. There was public outrage that this report had not been released before and demonstrations were organised all over the English-speaking world. The aliens watched it on television news channels and, although it meant that their secret was now well-known, they laughed and were well-fed.

Like many of the host mothers a girl called Sarah had become pregnant with an alien baby at the age of fifteen. Although she had protested to her family that she had not consented to sex but had been knocked out like Cathie, her father had chucked her out and she had ended up on the streets, stealing food to survive. She would go into a supermarket and eat what food she could find while going around the shelves and then leave without paying for anything.

Eventually, she landed up at a Salvation Army hostel, six months pregnant, starving and in need of a bed to rest on. Her foolish parents had been in their car whilst rowing over her. Not concentrating on the road ahead, they had crashed into a lorry which had killed them both instantly. So, Sarah had no family left that she knew of. She had never met her grandparents from either side as they had all died before she'd been born.

After a good night's rest, social services had been called and she had ended up in a not so good care home. At least now her skinny body was being fed and she had a place to sleep at night. At five feet ten inches tall, she had long legs, was a natural brunette with long brown hair and was a stunner but she was intelligent too. Apart from the reptilian rash, she had no idea that she was carrying an alien baby.

She went into a fourteen-hour labour in a darkened room alone and exhausted, she only saw the baby once it had made a human cry, so she still had no idea that it was an alien. At the age of sixteen, she had had to leave the care home and, while proper arrangements should have been made for her, she was literally turfed out onto the streets with her baby. She went to social services and was given a one-bedroomed flat in a high-rise tower where the lifts didn't work. Despite suffering from post-natal depression, she got a job as a part-time waitress. While she was at work, her baby was cared for at a nursery but he could vanish at will, move small objects without touching them and hurt his carers if he was told off. In the end, no nursery would take him so she had him adopted by some rich Americans who paid her well. Her only stipulations were that they would keep his name which was Daniel, would not tell him that he had been adopted and would send pictures of him every so often. The Americans were so desperate for a child that, despite their reservations, they readily agreed.

So, when Zygon summoned Daniel to England, he killed both his adopted parents before leaving. With all this alien activity, Sarah like the other host mothers found that she could contact Daniel and knew where he was. When Zygon found out, he was furious and caused Daniel a lot of pain by torturing him into agreeing to kill his real mother. Sarah was hoping to meet him and she was delighted when he suggested that they could meet up, if she came to visit him in South-East London.

With the money that the Americans had given her, Sarah had gone back to school, passed her exams and joined the Royal Air Force, rapidly qualifying as a pilot. She was currently 'on leave' and back in the UK, rehabilitating on a base in Yorkshire, as she had been shot in the arm in Afghanistan. She arranged to meet her superior, the wing commander, and asked him for some leave so that she could go and visit her son who had been adopted by an American family. Apparently, he was now living in a new estate in South-East London and she desperately wanted to explain why she had had to have him adopted. She bought a return train ticket to London and, when she arrived at Kings Cross, she took a taxi.

Daniel had suggested that they meet by the swings in a children's playground which was adjacent to the new estate. It was late in the afternoon when she arrived, but being autumn, it was getting dark when she walked into the deserted play area. She sat down on a bench to wait for her son then suddenly there was a storm of dust and out of it Daniel appeared. She recognised him from the photos she had been sent.

He didn't give her a chance to speak but lifted her up until she was high in the air and then turned her around and around. She could feel a splitting pain through her head and could hear him shout,

"I should have killed you in the first place".

For half an hour, he fed off her distress, before her heart stopped. He left her body in a ditch that ran alongside the bushes at the edge of the playground, covered it with leaves and then disappeared.

It was a few days later, when Sarah's commanding officer reported her missing, along with the fact that she had been going to visit her son who was apparently residing in the new estate in South-East London. The Metropolitan Police might not have paid that much attention to this report except that they had had a number of other reports detailing how some women had died suddenly, around the time their children had left home to move to the same estate. Even more curious was the fact that on paper most of the children involved were only five or six years old but, in reality, they appeared to be fully grown teenagers. So, the police organised a search of the surrounding area. When Sarah's body was discovered they started asking a lot of questions in the new estate. The news was leaked to the press and everyone was warned not to go near the place.

For once in his life, Zygon was a bit annoyed with himself. Perhaps his idea that the hybrids should kill their mothers so that their whereabouts would be concealed had backfired. In particular, he realised that he should have given Daniel much more specific instructions. Yes, kill his mother, but not in a location that would automatically lead the police to the new hybrid estate.

At the same time, it was clear to Zygon that his followers needed much more space. Some of the hybrids were mature enough to reproduce and had, by then, managed to have their own children and many of those who hadn't, had received hybrid babies or children from his moon spaceship.

Meanwhile Zygon's scientists had found a nerve gas that would paralyse and kill humans but not hurt the zygonites or hybrids. Zygon came up with a particularly dramatic plan. He decided to use the nerve gas on Moscow and its surroundings, spraying it using his small, cooched battleships which couldn't be detected by radar. The Russians were caught out by this totally unpredictable attack and most of the fifteen million humans in the area died very quickly, as the gas permeated into the air in their buildings.

The Russian President's voice was heard broadcasting just before he died. He said, "The gas came from Britain, blame Britain and its allies!"

Why Zygon had chosen Moscow nobody really knew. Russia is the largest country in the world and Zygon may well have thought that the distances between Moscow and other cities in Russia would make it relatively easy to defend. Furthermore, taking out the central federal government with the legislative, executive and judicial functions would create total chaos across the whole country. Russia was comprised of a large collection of semi-autonomous but disparate regions with communities who would struggle to communicate with each other, let alone join forces to regain control of Moscow.

The Russian ambassadors to the United Kingdom, France and the USA immediately resigned in protest and the twenty-four-hour news channels and the newspapers were full of the story for the next few days. After all it's not every day that a whole city is wiped out – let alone the capital city of one of the greatest powers in the world! Britain and America protested their innocence but people did not know what to believe. Yet again many feared that the world was on the brink of World War Three.

However, Zygon's attack had not only killed the President but also the Russian Defence Minister and their Chief of Staff. So, there was no one left with either the authority or the desire to launch a nuclear attack on the West and what good would it have served? There were a lot of meetings and negotiations behind closed doors. At the same time, although the rest of the world didn't know it, Moscow was being repopulated again: by hybrids!

While Zygon's plans were going well for him, one of the surviving host mothers, called Diana, arranged a meeting of the host mothers at a hotel on Silver Sands in Barbados, the resort where Pete and I had got married. Diana knew that Zygon had arranged the natural disaster that had killed her parents, while they were on holiday in the Philippines and she had inherited several million pounds. Consequently, she had the resources to pay for some of the poorer host mothers and their companions to stay, as they wouldn't have been able to come otherwise. Since Zygon was used to speaking in English by then, they all had known of the imminent attack on Moscow. However, most of them had been far too scared to inform the authorities, in case they would be punished for raising an alien child.

I joined Cathie in Barbados to give her moral support, leaving my much beloved husband and Rosie behind. After finishing her 'A' levels Cathie had attained a place at Southampton University to study Medicine with the hope of specialising in Obstetrics & Gynaecology. She had completed the first year of her degree, following a gap year, and wouldn't have been able to go to Barbados had the meeting not been conveniently scheduled within her Easter vacation.

The hotel staff were quite surprised to be suddenly fully booked in April but the women, posing as tourists, soon made friends and there was a large room where they could all meet privately to discuss their plans. In the end, they decided to send a delegation of five women, including Diana, to the White House, to tell the American President or one of his aides what they knew. They ended up talking to a General Howard and told him that they had known about the attack on Russia, that they were in telepathic contact with the zygonites and would be able to predict any of Zygon's plans to harm humans, in the future. Initially, General Howard thought they were all mad but the host mothers predicted the exact date and time of an earthquake in Tahiti which enhanced their credibility. NATO became involved and all the evidence was gathered including Sanderston's and Davidson's reports as well as the police reports of the missing teenagers and the murders of the mothers of the alien children.

This could well have been a good example of the world waking up far too late to the severity of the threat it was facing, as was clearly the case with both climate change and pollution. However, on this occasion, due to Colonel Turner's diligence combined with a generous budget allocation, the USA was well prepared to handle the crisis. Turner, himself, had become absolutely convinced of the existence of the aliens on Earth.

The British government secretly gave the US its blessing to test their satellite infra-red technology on the hybrids' estate in South-East London. This appeared to work well, although most of the aliens had left, they caught about a dozen around the flats in London. Their bodies were taken to a museum so everyone could see what they looked like. Many people were surprised and couldn't understand how they could look human while alive and alien when dead.

After that success, and with the approval of the six remaining Russian Federal Districts, most notably the North-western Federal District whose capital is St. Petersburg, NATO repeated the exercise over Moscow. The high intensity of the beam killed most of the hybrids there but a few who stayed under cover and avoided going outside or too close to windows survived. The host mothers had warned NATO that if Zygon was not in Russia or London at the time, the plan to drive them out completely might well fail, but they didn't listen.

As the host mothers had expected, Zygon and his family were not in Moscow but had been in his secret Colombian base at the time. Zygon was absolutely furious! Recognising that NATO was likely to follow up their attack on Moscow with a house to house search, he ordered the survivors to make their way to his base in Colombia while keeping their whereabouts secret. His temper was not improved when the UK and US governments enacted new laws decreeing that all babies who looked alien at birth, or whose fathers could not be identified as human, should be put in an infrared box. This wouldn't kill them if they were human but would if they were the offspring of zygonites.

Zygon was exceptionally gifted at telepathy. Not only could he use this power to broadcast his instructions to both the zygonites and hybrids and pick up any information they might have for him, he could also block off his thoughts so that nobody else would know about them. For instance, the police didn't know that Fred Barker was the aliens' leader and the host mothers had no idea of the whereabouts of his base on Earth.

Zygon had actually married a human woman, called Amba who had become a host mother after giving birth to their first son. The truth was that her own mother had been an addict and she had been abused as a child by her mother's numerous boyfriends. She had been just fifteen when Zygon, in human form, had accosted her in a bar and when he had suggested that she accompanied him to Colombia, she had been only too pleased to get away from her mother. Admittedly, in human form, Zygon was even older than the men that her mother had forced her to accommodate, but Amba was attracted by his apparent wealth and power.

From his point of view, initially, Amba had been just a means of propagating his hybrid race but he had found the process more pleasurable than he had expected. Whether this was just the realisation of an 'old man's dream' of having sex with a young, nubile girl or the fact that her previous experience helped him to enjoy their encounters was not totally clear. However, after their second son had been born, Zygon found that they had a particularly strong telepathic bond. This persuaded him to form a couplet with her.

When Amba had picked up the message about the host mothers' meeting in Barbados, she had told Zygon about it and, immediately, he had recognised the potential to be gained by Amba attending. She had no concern at all that, in agreeing to spy for Zygon, she might be betraying the human race as, given her experience, she didn't care for humans at all.

She had joined the other host mothers in Barbados and had kept Zygon informed as to what Diana's group were doing. He had not expected them to have any success with the US government but given what had happened, he was determined that they should be amongst the first to pay.

He knew that Amba had arranged a small party to visit the zoo in the North of the island one day so he chose that time to send two of his helicopters to bomb the Silver Sands resort. Cathie and I were fortunate to be in the group of survivors. Amba had planned to go to the zoo on her own but Cathie had insisted that we and a few others join her.

While Amba had not mixed particularly well with the other mothers, no-one had had even an inkling that she had a close relationship with Zygon. However, Cathie soon became suspicious of her. While the other host mothers had shared private information about their families and their work, Amba had been silent and aloof. When she had announced her trip to the zoo, I had remembered that Pete and I had been there just after our marriage some twenty-five years earlier. I had thought it would be interesting to go there again, so many years later and for Cathie to see some of the rest of the island. Cathie had thought that it would be a good way of getting to know Amba better.

When we went to the zoo, Cathie started to ask awkward questions, such as where she had come from and what had happened to her child. Afraid that her cover might be blown, Amba had contacted Zygon via telepathy. He had told her to separate herself from the group so she had gone into the zoo's washroom facilities. We had all waited outside for a long time but thinking that something might have happened to her, Cathie and I had gone inside to investigate. Amba wasn't there and had only left behind a small mirror with some grains of white powder on it. She seemed to have just vanished. Actually, Zygon had transported her back to the mansion in Colombia.

Cathie realised that the host mothers might be in danger and had tried to contact them but, by this time, Silver Sands had been bombed and all the host mothers who had been there were dead. The remaining host mothers mourned the loss of their friends, calling it an act of war and we concluded that Amba was a spy and that she was very close to Zygon – maybe even his wife.

Zygon's next step was to order his scientists to make protective clothing for his race to make them immune to infra-red light. While this was happening, a second small moon orbiting the Earth could be seen with an infra-red telescope. Zygon ordered most of the remaining aliens and hybrids to return there, arranging for a cooched cargo ship, with a large hold, to pick them up from his mansion in Colombia. All this was kept hidden from the remaining host mothers, including Cathie who still didn't know the whereabouts of his Earth base. At the same time, having lost a large quantity of his followers in Moscow, he also accelerated his programme of abducting female human teenagers to boost the production of hybrids.

Sanderston had died from a stroke initiated by the growth of his brain tumour but Davidson was still alive and he detected the new moon spaceship with his telescope. He told NATO about it and suggested that they act quickly to deal with both of the Mother Ships. The delegation of host mothers, who had previously contacted the US administration, had not been in

Barbados at the time of the bombing. So, they were able to tell NATO that the timing was right to attack the artificial moons, as Zygon and his family had gone back to one of the Mother Ships.

However, the American President wanted to negotiate a deal with the zygonites to live peacefully together so there was a delay but when he, eventually, understood that the zygonites lived on human distress and caused 'natural disasters', he changed his mind. They were obviously a serious threat to human existence.

So, NATO successfully targeted both moons with rockets armed with nuclear warheads which killed the zygonites, hybrids and all the human teenagers on board. There was a public outcry with regards to the loss of the teenagers but NATO defended its actions by saying that, if nothing had been done, even more teenagers would have been captured. At that time, Earth didn't have any spacecraft that could have rescued the young women.

Amba had been reporting back to Zygon everything that the host mothers were doing or were involved in. She had told Zygon that the two spaceships in the sky were going to be nuked but it wouldn't happen until the host mothers confirmed that he was on one of them. As a result, Zygon, his scientists, his generals, his senior politicians and some of the hybrids left just in time. Their smaller vessels were damaged by the nuclear explosions and crashed into the Atlantic Ocean but they were all transported back to Zygon's mansion in Colombia. A few small battleships and the large carrier spacecraft which he had used when he had arrived on Michael's farm, were cooched and waiting for them, on his land.

For the next five years there was no obvious sign of alien activity on Earth. The remaining host mothers stayed in contact by telepathy. They had mostly learned, like the aliens, to switch it on and off so their very private lives were still a secret. They all returned home and went back to their previous lives. Most people knew that there had been aliens on Earth, that their main ships had been destroyed by nuclear weapons and that NATO had been helped by the host mothers. So, instead of being shunned by their families and friends, they were honoured as heroines and most were welcomed back to their previous employment.

I went back to having a family life with my husband and two children with a part-time career as a riding instructor, running my own business, in the New Forest. Moscow started to be re-populated by humans and a new president of Russia, who had radical ideas, was elected. Cathie finished her Medical degree and embarked on her two-year registration posts. She was permanently tired, even though she was working either a partial week of days, followed by the same on nights. This was certainly less arduous than my registration had been.

"I know it was harder for you, Mum, but there are building works outside my hospital accommodation. They are making so much noise that I can't sleep during the day!"

"You should have told me dear. You can stay with us during your days off, after all, Lyndhurst is not so far away from Southampton. Your old room is full of junk but I can easily clear it out and drive you back to your hospital room when you are working on days. We promise that we will be as quiet as possible."

She took my advice and after her registration took a six-month break, before taking a post in Paediatrics as a prelude to embarking on a career in Obstetrics & Gynaecology. She felt that, after her experience, she would have more empathy with her patients. She also felt she would have no difficulty killing any alien babies, especially if their mothers had a reptilian rash.

In the meantime, Rosie had done a degree in Agriculture, at Reading University, specialising in Animal Husbandry. Then she had married Michael Woodman's son, Paul, and had joined the Woodmans on their farm. Everything else seemed to be going well. Although there were families still mourning for their female children, on the whole, the majority of people were, generally, glad that the alien moons had been destroyed and that the zygonites' threat to conquer the Earth was over.

But was it really over?!

Part 5

DILDA'S STORY

We will all remember the day when Marcus arrived on Alpha. It was a glorious, summer evening and the twin suns were just setting, lighting up the sky with a panorama of rainbow colours. We were sitting on the sand, around an open fire, eating. Dilda was looking especially lovely in her best blue dress and had used some of my make-up to cover the scars on her face. She had sustained these when alphan traitors had broken into her cave and had tortured her. They had wanted to get the co-ordinates of the bagaloo stores in the seabed for the megalattans but no co-ordinates existed, as the bagaloo was retrieved by magic. On this particular evening, she seemed unusually excited and whispered to me that something very special was going to happen tonight.

Then we heard the humming of engines and could see an unexpected spacecraft, heading towards us in the sky. We were all startled at first, except Dilda. In unison, we put down our plates to head for the safety of the caves but Dilda said,

"Don't be alarmed! It's only Marcus. He's my friend."

No-one knew of anyone called Marcus, so we stood and watched as the ship put down its landing gear and settled on the beach close by. The spacecraft was a little different from alphan ones with a long nose and four large sockets at the front for firing rockets, instead of lasers. The cockpit was small but it had a large rear section with a lack of windows so it looked like it had been used for carrying goods. Its shields for protection from the heat of re-entry, appeared to be made of a metal that we didn't recognise and it was not cooched. The shields had not been lifted by the pilot so we had no idea who was inside until the cockpit door slid back and he toppled out. Dilda was obviously concerned but couldn't reach him because of her chain which was there for own safety.

"Don't just stand there, please help him up."

So, Pete and I obliged. He looked like Dilda except that he was taller, more muscular with a bald head and no breasts. He was wearing brown breeches and a grubby white shirt. Suddenly, he was by Dilda's side and we looked on in wonder as he started to kiss her passionately. She gently pushed him away but held his hand and smiled. Then he noticed her chain and pointed at us, shouting and breaking it with his bare hands. Dilda spoke to him softly in a language which none of us had heard before and he seemed to calm down. Dilda held his hand and they walked towards us and we were introduced. Marcus sat down by the fire and Dilda got a plate full of bagaloo for him. He turned it into a strange, foul-smelling dish and devoured the lot in seconds, using his hands. She then took a bottle of wine, opened it and offered him a glass. He patted it away and it hit a rock, bursting into pieces. Then he grabbed the bottle and proceeded to drink directly from it, downing the whole lot. We sat down and continued eating in silence. Dilda spoke to him and he suddenly got up swept her into his arms and they disappeared.

Eventually, Cathie broke the shocked silence:

"Who is he?" she inquired but nobody knew.

"Well, obviously Dilda knows him but I always thought she was the last of her kind. She's got a lot of explaining to do," Moma Cara said. "And I think we had better wait for her return. I need some answers and I'm concerned about her safety."

About half an hour passed and I suggested that Pete and I should try to find her.

Just then a flustered Dilda returned, "I'm sorry about that. He's been travelling without food, drink and sleep for a week and he's now asleep in a bed in my quarters. I didn't expect him to behave quite like that but he now knows that I am not yet ready to..." Her voice trailed off.

"To have a romantic relationship," I interjected.

"Exactly," she exclaimed, and added, "Aptly put."

"Dilda, he's barbaric and you should have asked me before assuming he could stay. Well, you'll have to teach him some manners and Alphanese. We're not all going to learn his strange language," Moma Cara said sternly.

"I know, I'm sorry!" Dilda looked embarrassed and there were tears in her eyes. "I was not expecting his arrival to go quite as it did."

She composed herself, wiping her eyes and looking prepared to answer any questions from Moma Cara.

"How long have you known him?"

"Several years by telepathy but I didn't confide in anyone as, until a few days ago, I never thought that he would come here. He was too loyal to his master."

"Well, at least he has loyalty. So, what changed?" Moma Cara continued.

"His planet had a civil war and his master was killed. He only managed to escape, 'in the nick of time', by transporting himself to a free ship."

"And why was he so angry that he broke the chain?"

"It reminded him of the time when our race was enslaved. I should have warned him about it but I was too embarrassed to tell him that it was only there to stop me wandering off and getting into trouble. I will teach him and once you get to know him, I'm sure you'll find him acceptable. Please can he stay?"

"For the moment but will you be safe with him in your quarters? We all got the impression that he wanted more than you were prepared to give. He lost his temper very quickly with us and you will have to keep wearing a chain until we know him better."

"Of course, I'll be safe!" she exclaimed, "I have already explained to him about those very issues and I assure you it won't happen again."

"Well, it had better not!"

For the next few weeks Dilda stayed in her quarters with Marcus, only leaving him to collect heated bagaloo for the two of them, water and wine. When they next appeared, he was holding Dilda's hand and wearing long trousers and a T-shirt. He was courteous and apologised for his previous behaviour. Speaking fluent and polite alphanese, he introduced himself and immediately learnt all our names. He said it was a pleasure to meet us. When eating he chose a more conventional meal and used a knife and fork.

He spoke at length about his master and the planet Than which he had come from which was nearly four million light-years away. This was why it had taken him so long to get to Alpha, even with his ship's special time-travelling capabilities which meant that he could move very much faster than the speed of light. He seemed anxious to get to know us and was surprised when he learnt that Cathie was my daughter and Pete was my husband, as I looked like an alpha. He seemed very interested in the process of Embryolization. Dilda had told him about humanising solution which had been one of Mercia's most impressive innovations. However, he knew that this hadn't been readily available at the time the alphan scientist had taken my DNA to Earth and slipped it into my Earth mother's eggs. He offered the opinion that the scientist had been both brave and extremely skilful. He also suggested that it had been the inability to replicate his skill that was the probable cause of the failure of the later efforts at Embryolization.

We were all warming to him as Dilda had predicted and she seemed to be almost in awe of him. I noticed that her facial scars had gone and she explained that Marcus had used his magic to remove them, something that she had not been able to do for herself. I had never seen her so happy and was pleased for her. Towards the end of the evening he addressed Moma Cara,

"Please can I stay and please can Dilda's chain be removed completely so we can go for a walk in the long grass on the cliffs above. I do realise the reason for the chain now but I swear that I'll protect her and bring her back safely?"

Moma Cara hesitated, looking at us for inspiration, "Don't be away too long."

"Thank you very much, "he replied graciously.

Marcus started to take Dilda for short walks every day which she enjoyed but not having had much exercise for years, she often got tired and the couple would reappear with Marcus holding her in his arms. The relationship blossomed and we all grew to like him. He was deferent with Moma Cara and so kind and gentle with Dilda. He started calling her 'my love' and 'darling' and I noticed one day, in her cave, that they had changed their single beds into a king size double. On another occasion, I saw them passionately kissing on the sand.

They were obviously having sex but I was curious to know how they were managing it. So, one day when Dilda and I had both woken up early and were on the beach together, I said,

"Dilda, this is a very private question to ask and I will understand if you don't want to answer it but how do your people have sex?"

Then I hurriedly said,

"It's ok if you don't want to tell me and it's too personal to talk about."

Fortunately, she was happy to explain.

She said, "You fall in love first then a spare wire grows in the mechanical parts. We unscrew each other's front plates, much like taking each other's clothes off and then we connect these wires together."

"It is extremely pleasurable," she added, "And I am already pregnant! However, I don't want anyone else to know in case I miscarry."

"Your secret's safe with me. You know me, don't you?" I laughed, "Not one for idle gossip. How long will the pregnancy last?"

"About six months," she said.

Life carried on as normal and we continued to spend the summer on Alpha, knowing that any time we spent there would somehow not count on Earth. Although we'd be older, we would arrive on Earth about forty minutes after we had left. Although the cave we had was rented to us by Moma Cara, it was a cheap holiday for us and meant we could save more money for Rosie's and Cathie's futures.

One morning, I was taking a walk on the beach and noticed that it was unusually quiet for that time of day. The mopeds used by the cavens, as they were known to us, to get to work lay silent on the beach, outside their caves. Only a few alphas could transport themselves so most of them had some kind of vehicle to travel in or on and for the cavens it was mopeds. Most of the men worked in an ammunitions factory just outside Alpha's major city, Chaner, and most of the women worked in a weaving factory close by. They were paid every month with gold pieces that were weighed in cotton bags to make sure that the correct amount was given as the pieces were not all of the same size. It was an antiquated system and was time-consuming but for generations, it had been like this and no-one had thought of minted coins, like we had on Earth. The gold pieces were mined from Alpha's central desert and could be used to pay for commodities, such as installation of electricity into their caves so that the cavens could have lights, washing machines and cookers etc. This would be in keeping with the rest of the alphas who lived in houses in the cities. Of course, bagaloo was free and could be picked by anyone.

I wondered what had stopped them from leaving their caves and then I spotted three dragons lying on the sand by the sea. Initially, I was frightened as wild dragons could be fierce which was the obvious reason why the cavens had not ventured out. However, as an alphan child, I had been good with dragons so I rushed into our cave to get some heated bagaloo. When I approached them, slowly and cautiously, the grey male stood up. He was about fourteen feet high and when he spread his wings, the span was forty feet wide. His hind legs were like tree trunks but like the other two, he looked young and malnourished. For a moment, I thought that I was going to be burnt alive but he accepted the food and nudged the other two smaller palomino females to stand up and eat. The bagaloo was immediately changed into dragon food and devoured. They were so thin that I could see their ribs beneath their reptilian skin and they all had sores on their backs which would need treatment with a poultice from Dilda. One of the females had a larger belly than the others and I guessed that she might be pregnant.

Finally, the grey spoke to me telepathically in Megalonese, "Do not be afraid little alpha. We come in peace. Our master let us escape, when Megalatta was first hit and before the planet imploded into its sun. Using magic, we have travelled from planet to planet to find a home where we would be accepted and safe. Initially, there were fifty of us and we are the remaining three. Please let us stay. We just need a place to rest and gain strength."

"I will have to ask our Supreme Leader but as far as I'm concerned, you are welcome," I replied.

There was mucus dripping from the male's large nostrils. I took a hanky out of my pocket and wiped his long nose with it. He had red beady eyes and smaller front legs so was used to standing on his hind ones.

Everyone said how brave I had been and Moma Cara opened up a large cave for them. Dilda and Marcus went to a market and brought some hay to be stored and then used, gradually, to cover the stone floor to make them feel more comfortable. Although Marcus didn't speak Megalonese yet, he said that he and Dilda would look after them. I knocked on a few doors to tell the cavens that the dragons would be staying for a while but that there was nothing to fear and the word spread. Eventually, many cavens just came out and went to work.

We decided to go back to Earth and the New Forest the next day and carried on living our lives content and happy. We were called back to Alpha, five months later by Marcus who I realised was in telepathic contact with me as well. Dilda was in labour and because of her age she was struggling. I arrived to find that Marcus had taken off her front plate and saw that she had grown a compartment below her metal and wiring parts which was full of at least four little ones.

"When will we know when she is ready to deliver them?" I asked Marcus.

"When she's ready to push," he replied.

I had never seen Dilda so distressed before since the day she'd been tortured by alphan traitors. So, I mopped her sweaty face with clean, cold water and set up some gas and air for her to breathe, to ease the pain. By then, the contractions were coming every three minutes. Eventually, after a few hours, she was ready to push and out came six of them. Their tiny bodies looked just like Marcus and Dilda and were removed to a cradle. However, despite being exhausted, Dilda wanted to breast-feed and hold them all, which she did before falling asleep. Marcus was relieved as his children were all ok except for the last one who was struggling to breathe and briefly needed additional oxygen. I stayed on for a few days to make sure that Dilda and her little ones were doing well. They started to grow very fast and were born potty trained so they didn't need nappies. Dilda was exhausted every day from breast-feeding them but Marcus would give them bottled milk while she was sleeping. So, I returned home.

Six months later, I tried to contact Dilda to ask if Cathie and I could come and visit but got Marcus instead. Moma Cara agreed and, having locked up our house, we were with them in twenty minutes. I was amazed that Dilda's children had grown up so quickly and were playing pat ball (a sort of badminton), albeit with a lower net than was used by older children. Dilda was sitting near them on the sand outside their home and keeping a watchful eye on them.

Basically, the children were like Dilda and Marcus only smaller but like any children they needed time off from studying and time to play. All the girls were identical and wore short floral dresses. The boys didn't look the same but were all dressed in blue T-shirts and shorts. Unfortunately, they could not go swimming in the sea, as the salt would have rusted their mechanical parts.

When we arrived, Fred and George complained that I'd forgotten to feed them again. A box of bagaloo was immediately heated up for them by Moma Cara which, once it had cooled, turned it into Walkers plain crisps and Fred and George scoffed the lot.

I was surprised that the children had grown up so fast but, apparently, this was natural for their race. Dilda explained that it had been an evolutionary path. Her race had been peaceful but kept being attacked by aliens who killed all the babies or took them away to be slaves. So, they had learnt to grow up fast to protect themselves. To my astonishment, they also all recognised me and gave up their game to come over for a hug.

The local school had refused to take them so they were being tutored at home. Their alphanese was remarkable but they were also being taught their native tongue and all of them could read and write. There were three of each sex and the girls played against the boys. The girls usually won as, at this age, they were stronger and fitter than the boys. Also, the runt of the litter was male and was noticeably smaller than the rest of them. I felt for him, as I had been the last of Moma Bara's sextuplets to be born. I had spent the first three months of my life in hospital and I was always smaller than the rest of my siblings.

The cave next to Dilda's had been an office for Moma Cara but she had moved out to the next cave along and a hole had been put in the wall between the caves. So, the children had an area for themselves which was connected to their parents' living quarters. Everything seemed to be going so well and I was pleased for Dilda and Marcus.

In fact, they had planned to get married the very next day and I helped Dilda to get ready. Something had changed in her and she looked radiant. However, this happiness was not going to last long and no-one could have predicted the disaster that was coming next!

A few days later, Cathie rushed up to me while I was picking bagaloo from one of the large trees near the sand.

"You look flustered dear." I said, "Whatever is the matter?"

"Mum, please listen, this is important. Come into our cave with me," she whispered. "Zygon is still alive and he knows about Dilda's children. He is sending his Chief General, Aroneus, to abduct them to use them as his slaves."

"What?" I exclaimed, "How did the zygonites know?"

Looking shamefaced at me, she admitted that she had been so excited by their arrival that she had inadvertently broadcasted that information.

"Cathie, I know that you are new to telepathy and your connection with the zygonites has been most useful but I told you that it works both ways?" I shouted, "How long have we got?"

"Please don't be mad at me Mum. I'm so sorry. I didn't mean this to happen" she sobbed

"How long?" I repeated

"Just a day, maybe."

"Well, you will have to tell Marcus and Dilda as this is all your fault!"

Just then there was a knock at the door. Marcus, having heard the shouting, came in.

"Tell us what?" he inquired.

Cathie tried to answer but was so distressed that she wasn't making sense so I told Marcus. His reaction was surprising, he went pale, sat down, bent over with his head in his hands and said nothing. His silence was more unbearable for Cathie, than the shouting. Eventually he spoke.

"Dilda will be devastated!"

Then turning to me he asked, "Would the High Council allow us to use alphan weapons?"

"I doubt it," I replied solemnly. "You and Dilda are not popular amongst the alphas and using alphan weapons would be tantamount to declaring war. Even if the answer was positive, it could take weeks for the High Council to come to a decision."

"Then we must do our best on our own. Will you help me?"

"Of course, I promise," I replied.

Then addressing Cathie, he commanded, "Tell Zygon that you are distressed because Alpha won't defend my family and then, young lady, I want you to return to Earth immediately."

"I'll take you on the hopper and come back. I'll only be away for forty minutes," I said, then added, "Marcus, you must tell Moma Cara to move to her residence in the country. There is nothing she can do here and hopefully she'll be safe there."

We set off on the hopper. I was a little concerned for Cathie's safety now that Zygon would know that she was in telepathic contact with him. However, she reassured me that Zygon wasn't on Earth anymore, having gone to a planet called Crema. I also hoped that because Cathie's message had come from Alpha that he would spare her, thinking that she might be a useful tool. I wondered what the zygonites were doing on Crema but Cathie didn't know.

Marcus went to find Moma Cara and apparently, after she had agreed to leave her cave, she wished him luck. Marcus then returned to his cave to tell Dilda. She had burst into tears and was inconsolable. Marcus had hugged her and promised to keep the family safe. A space in her inner cave was made. It was protected by a security system and Dilda and her children hid there. Although the zygonites might have been able to transport themselves into this space, they would not have immediately known that it was there and therefore, it would have given Marcus more time to change his plans, if necessary.

Then he went to his battered spacecraft. Turning on the ignition he found that the battery was still working as the dashboard lit up. However, he tried several times to lift off but to no avail. So, he got out and with his considerable powers of transportation, lifted the whole ship up and turned it around in the air. It came to rest on the sand, with its back just beyond Dilda's cave and the front, where his rockets were positioned, facing the sea. Then he waited.

It was late afternoon when I returned. He greeted me with a hug and we both got into the cockpit.

"I have four rockets," he said. "But I will need to use one to check that the mechanism is working."

I nodded and he fired the rocket. There was a loud explosion as the rocket plunged into the sea. We were overjoyed but a large crowd of cavens had approached the ship to complain about the noise. I got out of the cockpit to address them.

"We are expecting unwelcome visitors and had to test one of the rockets."

"What are you doing with that creature?" one of them yelled.

"Marcus is my friend and is Dilda's husband, so I am helping him to defend his family."

"Whose Dilda?" the trouble-maker asked.

"You know," I replied as calmly as I could. "The Prime Intelligence who helps Moma Cara."

"Where is she? I want to complain."

"She's in a safe place. Now there will be some more noise when the visitors arrive which won't last long. Collect supplies of bagaloo and stay in your homes until it's all over."

"You mean we're not safe," he yelled again.

"Look, I am Astra who once saved our people from the megalattans. Now I'm going to save Dilda's family from them. They are only interested in her children. You will be perfectly safe if you stay in your caves."

"First dragons, now this!" he complained but the crowd eventually dispersed.

"I knew there would be trouble," Marcus said. "That's why I waited for your return. I have told Dilda that I will be sleeping and eating in the ship. Will you stay with me? There are bathroom facilities at the back but nothing to heat up bagaloo."

Looking at the fear in his eyes, I was persuaded. So, I stayed and we waited. When Alpha's twin suns were just setting, I went inside the cave to get some heated bagaloo. Just then the zygonite ship arrived on the sand quite close to the sea. It was cooched and silent apart from a slight humming of its engines. Aroneus must have transported himself and some robots onto the sand, without opening the ship's doors. Consequently, they seemed to appear suddenly from nowhere. I could hear Marcus shouting in my mind so I dropped the bagaloo, grabbed my infra-red gun and rushed outside. I fired at Aroneus and one of the robots fired back, catching me on my right flank. I screamed as the pain shot through me. Marcus transported me into the cockpit.

"That was stupid," he shouted. "Can't you see he's clad in protective clothing."

Then in a gentler voice, "Are you badly hurt? Are you ok to stay?"

"Yes," I gasped, "It's painful but I think I'll be alright."

"Good. What's he saying?"

"He's sorry about the robot's actions but they are trained to protect him. He says that he comes in peace and only wants one of Dilda's sons and one of her daughters."

"That's enough!" Marcus exclaimed, positioning a rocket and then firing.

The rocket went straight through Aroneus, killing him instantly and going on to hit the cooching device of his ship so we could see it break in two. More zygonites and robots appeared. They were slowly moving towards us, when Marcus fired again taking out a group of them and hitting the ship's fuel tank. The ship exploded and the enemy was temporarily flattened but most of them got up and continued to advance. Marcus tried to fire the third rocket but the mechanism jammed. By then I had lost a lot of blood and was drifting in and out of consciousness. However, in a lucid moment I asked myself what I would have done when, as Astra, I had saved the alphas so many years ago. Then the idea came to me.

"We've failed," Marcus wept. "Dilda and I will be found and killed and the children will be taken away in a carrier ship to be slaves! I suppose I could transport us all to the top of the cliffs but we'll still be defenceless."

"Definitely not yet, put up all your shields and turn on the video link with the outside. I'm going to summon the dragons," I managed to whisper.

I said the short, megalattan spell and we waited. The robots had started cutting through the metal of the cockpit doors with their lasers and we could hear the drilling sound, as the metal was being torn apart. I said the spell again, with a more urgent tone and suddenly two dragons burst out of their cave and took flight. Roaring flames came out of their open jaws and smoke came out of their nostrils. The drilling stopped as the robots left the doors and started to fire at the dragons but their dragon skin proved to be impervious to the lasers. The dragons hesitated as they had had a kind megalattan keeper and did not immediately recognise the megalattans now zygonites as the enemy.

Mustering all my strength, I screamed at the dragons, via telepathy, "Now, rid the beach of the robots and the megalattans and save us."

The dragons, already incensed by the enemy fire, obeyed. I remember seeing the absolute carnage. The zygonites were burnt to a crisp and the robots melted to pools of metal on the sand. Then I passed out.

The next thing I was aware of was opening my eyes and, for the first minute, everything was a blur. Eventually, I focused and saw that Pete was sitting next to me reading a book.

"Pete" I said in a cracked voice, "Where am I?"

"You're awake," he exclaimed. "How do you feel?"

"A bit sore. Where am I?" I repeated.

"You're in a bed in Dilda's cave," he replied.

"How long have I been asleep?"

"About a month."

"How did you get here?"

"Dilda contacted Cathie by that telepathy thing you all seem to have and we came in Michael's buggy but Michael had to go back to his farm."

"But Marcus banished Cathie."

"Everything is fine between them now and Cathie was needed to give blood for your transfusion. Dilda thought a mixture of human and alphan blood would be best."

"Thank God Cathie's still alive and the children?"

"They are safe and being tutored by Dilda, at the moment. Cathie says that Zygon has given up his quest to abduct them now that Alpha has resident dragons."

"And the dragons. Whose looking after them?"

"Why, Marcus, of course, and he has learnt to speak Megalonese so he can communicate with them. He says these dragons don't speak but he can read their minds like you can. He is so grateful for their help that he sneaks in extra bagaloo for them and thinks the rest of us don't know. The one, that did not respond to your call for help is lying at the back of the cave as she is heavily pregnant. Now that is enough questions for now. Dilda will tell you about your op. You must rest."

I closed my eyes. I did feel weak and tired and must have dozed off.

The next time I woke up, Cathie was sitting beside me.

"Mum, I'm so sorry for causing your injury," she sobbed.

"Cathie don't cry. You made a mistake but my injury was my own fault. I shot at Aroneus and one of his robots shot back. Thank you for coming back and donating some of your blood."

"It was the least I could do," she said, wiping the tears from her eyes. "So, you're not mad at me anymore?"

"No, dear. Come here and give me a hug"

"Oh Mum, we've all been so worried about you."

Then Dilda entered the room. "Enough of that young lady. I don't want the stitches to break. Cathie, I need to talk to your mother alone. Do you mind?"

"Of course not. I'll come back later."

Once Cathie had gone, a serious expression clouded Dilda's face.

"Do you realise you nearly died. I had to resuscitate you twice. Your right kidney was damaged beyond repair and had to be removed and your renal artery was severed. If you had been in human form you would have bled to death in the spaceship. Why didn't you get Marcus to transport you inside before?" she scolded.

"You're obviously cross with me but I promised Marcus I would help and he wouldn't have been able to summon the dragons at that time. The zygonites would have taken the children away and killed the rest of us," I said defensively.

"How could I be cross with you when you risked your life to save my family? Marcus and I will be eternally grateful to you," she said, her tone of voice softening.

"And I am grateful to you for saving my life with the operation. That makes us quits, yes?"

She nodded and said, "Now you should eat. I'll bring you your favourite chicken soup."

"Thank you Dilda. I am absolutely starving."

A few days later, Dilda arrived in my room and woke me up.

"Time to get moving," she commanded.

She gently removed my urinary catheter and my nappy which, thankfully, was clean this time. Then she removed the bandages to take the stitches out and I looked at the wound, for the first time. In dismay, I thought to myself will Pete still want me with this hideous scar? Dilda read my mind as usual:

"Don't worry Astra, Marcus will use his magic to remove the scar. He's already removed Cathie's and, apparently, she was ecstatic with the results," she said, as she cut the stitches.

Then she gave me some of my clothes to wear and helped me to put them on.

"You can have a shower tomorrow, if you can manage to walk."

Once I was dressed, Marcus appeared. It was the first time I'd seen him since the battle and he had a guilty expression on his face.

"I'm so sorry I should have…."

"Marcus don't! "I interrupted. "I made a promise and I always keep my promises. Anyway, it was entirely my fault. Now, Dilda has told me you have a spell for scars."

Marcus lifted up my T-shirt and placed his large, chubby hands on the wound. Then he whispered some words in his native tongue and removed his hands. The scar had started to fade.

"By tomorrow it will have gone," he said.

I thanked him and seeming embarrassed, he left immediately.

Dilda said "I'm sorry about that. He feels guilty for not helping you when you were bleeding so heavily."

"That's nonsense! I told him that I was alright."

"Just give him some time. He will eventually feel comfortable with you again," she reassured. "Now, let's see if you can walk?"

I got out of bed and took a few steps. It was painful but manageable so I took a few more, then had to go back to bed.

"Keep practising," she said "You're going to be fine."

A week later, I was woken up by a howling noise. Knowing immediately that the pregnant dragon had gone into labour, I put on my slippers and dressing gown and moved, as quickly as I could, to the dragons' cave. Marcus was already there comforting her. I gathered from him that she would die if she didn't manage to get her egg out soon. I turned to the Grey and asked if I could examine her. He nodded and I reached inside. The egg was too large to pass. When the next contraction came she pushed, tearing her flesh and adding blood to the pool beside her.

"You must pant, don't push next time, just pant."

She nodded. Then I turned to Marcus, "I need a sharp sterile knife and some dissolvable stitches."

"What are you going to do, you can't hurt her!" Marcus exclaimed.

"Her flesh is tearing and a clean cut will be easier to stitch and will heal much better than torn flesh."

Marcus disappeared and quickly returned with the items.

"Thank you," I said "What's her name?"

"Sara," he replied.

"Ok, Sara. You're going to feel a sharp pain down below," I said using telepathic contact.

Quickly doing the episiotomy, I reached in and managed to feel the top of the enormous egg.

"Now, Sara, I want you to push while I pull."

It took a few pushes but eventually a large egg was delivered then a smaller one came out. The Grey nudged the eggs to Sara's nostrils while I stitched her up. She blew a little fire onto them and they cracked, revealing twins in the first egg. Although Sara was obviously worn out, she licked her three babies until they wriggled and cried. Both Marcus and the Grey thanked me and I was just about to leave when the troublemaker from the other day arrived.

"What's all this noise, waking us up in the middle of the night? I can see it's you two again. Always the same culprits!"

"Sara was in labour. Didn't your wife scream when she was in labour?"

"Well, I suppose so but keep the noise down so decent folk can sleep," he said, looking at the baby dragons.

"They are cute, aren't they?"

"Well I suppose … as dragons go they are," he said. Then walked off muttering to himself.

"Well, I'm glad you were here to help Sara and deal with that dreadful peasant," Marcus laughed, relieved that the whole ordeal was over.

"Well, you were pretty barbaric when you first arrived."

"But not stupid!" He laughed again.

Then, turning to the Grey, I told him to allow Sara to rest, that the stitches that I had used would dissolve and not to mate with her for at least a month. He nodded and I went back to bed.

Marcus apparently heated up some bagaloo which the Grey turned into baby food and fed the tiny creatures. Marcus had slept in the dragons' cave that night which annoyed Dilda but she was furious when she learned that I had been allowed to help with the delivery.

However, when she saw the baby dragons, her heart melted and her mood changed. It seemed that everyone else felt the same.

Some weeks later, when the word had again spread, the caven children came to play with Sara's infants. She was apprehensive at first and watched their activities closely. I looked in Moma Bara's old store cupboard, which was in Dilda's cave. I found some toys that they could sensibly play with which I had provided for baby dragons before. I gave them to the baby dragons but they didn't know what they were at first. However, they soon learnt how to use them with the help of the caven children.

What were we going to do with the dragons now that they had a growing family? They were using up a lot of bagaloo and Marcus was given the task of mucking them out each day. At least the cavens chipped in, as they thought that dragon dung would make the bagaloo trees, in their gardens, grow and flower all year long. So, Marcus started charging a box of bagaloo, as a form of alphan currency, for each wheelbarrow full of dung but this could not be sustained and Marcus was getting exhausted.

So, we all came up with a plan for the dragons to go to the North of the planet, where a hardier type of bagaloo grew all year round. The rugged terrain and cold winters had put the alphas off from living there. I went to speak to the Grey about it but he already knew and he agreed to our plan and said that they would leave for the North, as soon as Sara's children could fly.

However, he added that if we ever needed their help again, we should just call them. So, I taught Marcus the summoning spell and, now that I was fit to travel, Cathie, Pete and I got on the hopper and returned home to Earth.

Part 6

ZYGON'S STORY

My family and the Woodmans will always remember the day when we could see what looked like a new, artificial moon, hovering in the stratosphere over London. It was about five years after the human race had thought that they were rid of the zygonites. Within minutes, the main television channels were carrying reports of similar sightings from all the capitals of the countries in the G20. After that, additional new moons were spotted above the other major population centres in the English-speaking world: New York, Los Angeles, Chicago, Miami and Houston in the USA, Toronto and Vancouver in Canada, Sydney and Melbourne in Australia and the Manchester conurbation in England. Any vestige of doubt as to who was responsible vanished when female adolescents started to go missing again.

The moon ships were much smaller than the alien moons that had visited Earth before but there were now thirty of them. They had been cooched while travelling from their origin on Crema, until they had taken up their positions over Earth. So, it seemed to the human race that they had all suddenly appeared from nowhere. The ones over Beijing and Washington DC were a little larger and red in colour. As they were different, they were known as the Mother Ships but they were actually command centres and home to the Zygon elite. It was impossible to use nuclear weapons to attack any of the ships, as they were far too close to the Earth's surface and the radioactive fall-out would have been catastrophic. The USA was one of the first countries to fire missiles with conventional warheads at them. This was met by extremely accurate laser fire and the rockets were blown to pieces, almost immediately after they had left the Earth's surface, damaging the bases from whence they had come.

It was clear that the zygonites had returned and some of the other host mothers became aware that quite a large number of zygonites and their hybrids had escaped the attack on Moscow. They had fled to Crema where they still had had the equipment and materials required to build the new ships. What they had needed but didn't have had been stolen from other nearby planets and the zygonites had killed their inhabitants, feeding off their distress.

Fred Barker's mansion in Colombia, which was protected by high security, had been identified by the police. They thought that he was implicated in drug running but they had never been able to catch him in the act and they certainly had no idea that he was the leader of the zygonites. The only people that knew were Amba, the rest of his family and members of his elite circle and they had been threatened to keep it secret or face death. Barker had been able to hide his true identity from everyone else, including the remaining host mothers. Had that not been the case, it would have been relatively easy to have bombed his mansion, killing both him, his family and any of his staff who were based there.

Zygon had been pleased with Amba after she had returned from Barbados. Aided by the ready availability of cocaine, their sex life had been good for the next couple of years, until he had started making trips to Crema to supervise the work going on there. On these occasions, their eldest son had taken over managing the drug business. Amba missed Zygon when he was away: it wasn't that she loved him, it was more that she felt much safer when he was around. Like the other hybrids, her boys had grown up very quickly and had very little respect for their mother. They were almost naturally inclined to bully her at every opportunity - after all, upsetting their human mother was a bit like having a snack. However, like everybody else, they were frightened of their father so they were careful not to treat Amba too badly when he was around.

As Zygon's absences became longer, the boys had bullied her more, and she'd used increasing doses of cocaine to bolster her mood. When the effect of this appeared to have diminished, she'd started to drink heavily as well. When Zygon had returned from his third trip to Crema, he'd rapidly lost interest in her. She was looking gaunt, haggard and had aged considerably – certainly she no longer provoked his libido in the way the nubile fifteen-year-old had done.

A few days later, high on cocaine, she had literally had enough and left the mansion to visit a local bar where she'd made the mistake of getting very drunk. Unfortunately, for both her and the zygonites, she had shared a table with a reporter. He had plied her with drinks and, eventually, she'd revealed that she was a host mother. Then she'd voiced the opinion that Zygon, the aliens' leader, was still alive and was planning to destroy the human race because of what they had done to his people in both London and Moscow.

She had refrained from identifying Fred Barker as Zygon and most people, who knew what she had said, had thought that her statement was merely the ravings of an intoxicated addict. However, Zygon had been outraged by her betrayal and couldn't risk any further outbursts from her. Effectively, Amba had signed her own death warrant. Zygon had duly obliged. Amba's children had not been at all upset. Indeed, they'd wanted to hear all the gory details so that they could feast on their mother's plight. Zygon, himself, had just rekindled his fantasy with another nubile fifteen-year-old, an Amba lookalike, named Seta.

The appearance of the new moons and their apparent indestructability had Zygon's desired effect. The human race panicked! People rushed and queued to take their savings out of their bank accounts, forcing many banks to fail. The Bank of England and its counterparts put up interest rates but it was not enough to stop hyperinflation. Stock market prices fell rapidly and eventually crashed. Wall Street was the first and then the others followed, as people started manically selling their stocks and shares and then fleeing to more rural areas, where they thought they would be safer. Michael even showed a little of his old, selfish, megalattan greed and bought some shares at very low prices. People were moving out of the affected cities as fast as they could to escape the moons overshadowing them, creating 'ghost towns' but nowhere was safe.

In an effort to contain the widespread terror, the Chinese and American Presidents, simultaneously, expressed the desire to negotiate a peace settlement with Zygon and promised that they would find a way to do this. However, about halfway through their speeches, and in front of the eyes of their audiences, they both inexplicably vanished. When they did not return, many politicians were deterred from speaking out. Zygon's scientists had discovered the ability to teleport humans to the moons without using intermediary spacecraft. Maybe they had had access to Mercia's book of spells, when they had abducted Sonja. It was called the 'captivation technique' and was poorly understood by the human race.

Zygon still planned to create a hybrid race. He targeted English-speaking, human adolescents mainly from Australia, the USA, Canada and Britain, as English was the only human language he had bothered to learn. Most people stayed indoors as much as possible and there had been a rise in home tutoring, as all the schools were closed. However, a fit, English-speaking, fifteen-year-old would be sitting with her family at home and would just vanish. When Zygon had learnt that laws had been passed world-wide to ensure that all alien babies were put into infra-red light boxes, he had been furious. He countered by making sure that this time all of the hybrids were born on his ships. Over the course of the following year, nearly one thousand more teenagers were abducted. The zygonites just ate up the girls' terror and ignored their protestations, feeding off their distress.

Then, to make matters worse, key staff at power stations just vanished. Initially, army soldiers took over their posts but when they met the same fate, nobody wanted to take their place. Without power, the technology that the world had relied upon for decades and had taken for granted was useless. Once batteries had run down there was no life in the internet, Facebook, e-mails or mobile phones. In Britain, this included the Social Security computers so those who had relied on social or disability benefit all their lives and had never saved had no money. Local shops and markets soon ran out of supplies so food distribution centres were set up. The hospitals ran for a while on back-up generators but people had to queue for hours to buy a loaf of bread or to be seen in A&E departments. Now, they had to pay an exorbitant amount of cash for both, money that many people could not afford. The gap between the haves and the have-nots grew ever wider, especially throughout all populations of the Western World. When the back-up generators eventually ran out of fuel, governments and police forces were decimated, creating lawless societies and putting everyone left in peril. All overseas grants to the poorer countries of the world stopped. When the charities working in these countries ran out of funds, many people, who were already suffering, just died.

Those that were hungry and had stayed in the major cities tried rioting on the streets but it was in vain. The mothers who had lost their children joined them but there were no governments or policemen left to support or hinder them. All the restaurants, supermarkets and their chains of supply were raided until there was no food left, except on the farms. However, farmers were having to manage without technology and electricity as well and, in general, they had to go back to ancient methods. Now, there was no reason why gangs wouldn't kill them for the food that they had produced.

Zygon's scientists had invented a complex machine that could store human distress electromagnetically. So, every moon had one. Zygon was a megalomaniac: as such, he had fanatical plans for the future. He dreamt of destroying the human race completely by using his nerve gas and feeding his ever-growing population of adult hybrids for thousands of years just by giving them a daily shock from one of the new machines. He could only see a few obstacles to overcome. He had to abduct enough female teenagers, cause plenty of 'natural' disasters to store human distress and then, in the absence of humans, take over the power supplies and the farms to provide enough food for the hybrid youngsters. He would have to wait until he had more mature adults who could reproduce but, for the moment, he was content to steal from the farms, to feed the captured teenagers and then the infant hybrids. He was confident, as the appearance of his new moons, his captivation technique and the resulting loss of power had helped him achieve his first two objectives. As he had expected, the general behaviour of most humans in a crisis of such magnitude had been a great asset.

Both my family and Michael's had survived, although his farm had been broken into many times and livestock had been taken. In his anger, he stayed up late one night and with his rifle, killed all the members of the gang who had been raiding the farm. They were buried, en masse, in a deep hole that the family had dug, in one of Michael's fields. It was filled in with earth and the turf with long grass growing from it was carefully put back on top to hide the grave. As there were no police around, Michael thought he would get away with it and it certainly stopped the raids on his farm. My family knew about the killings but none of us thought there would be any trouble. The families of the gang members protested and there were a few attempts to kill Michael, which fortunately failed. While Michael continued to produce food for everyone in his village and his friends, the rest of the population starved unless they could beg, buy or steal from a farmer in their area.

However, this could not be sustained. In particular, without her regular medication, Sonja was descending into a psychotic depression and needed Dilda's help. Michael, Sonja, David, Cathie and I decided to go to Alpha for help. Paul and Rosie were left behind to run the farm and Pete was supposed to prevent my ponies from being stolen. Moma Cara agreed to our visit and found us a cave to live in, while Dilda gave Sonja the alphan equivalents of the medication that she desperately needed. The cavens recognised me as Astra and when they heard that our planet was being destroyed by megalattans, now called zygonites, they wanted to help us.

Initially, there was no point in trying to rescue the teenagers as there was no accommodation or hospital services left on Earth to support them. So, our first aim was to find and kill Zygon. From Cathie's telepathic contact, we realised that Zygon was totally in command and that all the others, even his generals were afraid of him. We hoped that they were not used to thinking for themselves but were only able to take orders. So, our intention was to cause disarray amongst the zygonites, by destroying the source of their orders. However, we needed an alphan spacecraft to do this so we asked Moma Cara for her help.

"I can't put any alphan lives at risk but I will ask the High Council to vote on lending you a space battleship but obviously you would have to learn to pilot it yourselves," she said.

The High Council voted unanimously to lend us a battleship. With the exception of Sonja who was too sick, the rest of us decided to learn to pilot it and it took six months of intensive training to pass our tests. However, we succeeded in learning how to pilot all the different types of alphan spacecraft. Although there was not really much difference between alphan and zygonite battleships, Dilda said that she would do her best with her magic to alter it so it looked like a zygonite ship and protect it from fire. Dilda also provided us with lasers in case there were humans, working on board the Mother Ships and, of course, infra-red weapons and showed us how to fire them. She took me to one side and gave me her magic charm on a chain to wear around my neck.

"If you have to use a spell," she whispered, "Remember three things. Ask 'The Lord of Light' to help you not 'The Lord of Darkness' as Mercia would have done, remember the 'Law of Rebound' and you can say a spell or spells in English, if you prefer, the charm will adapt."

"Thank you, Dilda. This will be really helpful!"

Cathie informed us that there were no teenage captives on the Mother Ships and, consequently, all of the zygonites on board were in native form, except for Zygon's hybrid children. It was nearly the time when Michael and David would be needing another shot of the humanising depot, so it was just allowed to wear off and they returned to megalattan form overnight. Although, in many ways the zygonites were very different from our megalattan friends, it was fortunate that their physical form was just the same.

David volunteered for the first mission. He thought that Michael might be recognised, from the time when Zygon had asked for a ransom for Sonja's release, although

Michael had been in human form at the time. Cathie could visualise the clothes that the zygonites were wearing and was able to show Dilda a picture of them, by telepathy. So, Dilda made a uniform to fit David who intended to pose as an army zygonite. I decided to join him along with Cathie who had to come with us, as only she would be able to lead us to Zygon and identify him.

"It's a risk that I am willing to take," she'd said with a brave voice.

Preparations over, we got into the small alphan battleship and headed for Earth. David was the pilot and we hid behind the pilot's seat so that we would not be seen. The others stayed behind on Alpha. We flew to the moon over Washington DC first as Cathie reckoned that Zygon was there. David got us access to the landing bay, by lowering our ship's shields and showing himself to the keeper of the inner gate. Once inside, he got out of the ship and walked to the keeper's control room.

"Zygon has asked me to leave a package with you which he will personally pick up later," he said.

The keeper's powers of telepathy were not strong and, as Zygon flitted between the two Mother Ships and his mansion in Colombia, the keeper was often unaware of his exact whereabouts. He was also tired, as it was getting to the end of his shift, and so did not ask too many awkward questions. David was allowed to leave the package with him which, although small, contained a powerful, highly explosive, alphan bomb.

Just as we were leaving, Cathie sensed that Zygon had already transported himself without the package to the moon over Beijing, so we had just missed him. However, once we were back in space, we decided that even if it warned Zygon that there could be a traitor in his army, we would go ahead and detonate the bomb. The Mother ship over Washington DC was blown to pieces.

Having returned to Alpha, David transported us back to his cave where he had to stay with Michael as they couldn't risk being seen by the cavens, in megalattan form. We were worried as Cathie could confirm that David and our ship had been seen on CCTV. This had automatically and simultaneously been seen on the other Mother Ship's monitors because of the connection between the two command centres. A photo of David and our ship had been issued to Zygon, had been distributed to all his people and he had now been warned that the moon over Beijing, might well be our next target.

We had to come up with a better plan to trap Zygon and his family. Zygon considered returning to his mansion on Earth but his Chief Intelligence Advisor did not believe there would be another zygonite traitor and that they would recognise David and his ship, if he tried again. Michael desperately wanted to kill Zygon himself, so we decided to take the risk and let him pilot the ship the next time. However, we needed to change the identification number on it. Fortunately, the High Council had no objection to us doing this.

So, Michael in megalattan form was able to get Cathie and I onto the other Mother Ship over Beijing. Michael transported himself to the area in the landing bay where most of the smaller ships were stationed. He then secretively placed an active grenade near to them, before immediately returning to our ship. Although the zygonite ships had shields to go through re-entry into any planet's atmosphere, when they were at rest with their shields down they were very vulnerable to fire. When the grenade went off, the fuel in the zygonite ships ignited. There were several, relatively small explosions and the landing bay became full of smoke and fire.

This caused the zygonites to run around madly trying to put it out and provided us with good cover. Dilda had protected our ship from fire with her magic and, having cooched it, Michael transported us all to the main corridor that connected the landing bay to the interior of the Mother Ship. Once inside the main corridor, Cathie knew exactly where to find Zygon. We turned down a few corridors, blindly following her but Michael and I both expressed the feeling that it seemed like we were totally lost in a maze.

"We're close," Cathie said confidently, "Just one more corridor to go down."

However, we began to think that setting off the grenade in the landing bay had been a mistake, as the zygonites had not been able to contain the fire or explosions. The Mother Ship was falling apart, was on fire and the ceilings in the corridors were falling down all around us. There was a wall of flame behind us and one in front. I was in human form and so none of us could walk through the fire without getting burnt but Cathie and Michael were especially frightened.

"Why don't we just place a bomb here and I'll transport us back to our ship?" Michael said sweating profusely and looking terrified.

"No," I exclaimed. "We want to make sure that he doesn't escape this time."

"Well, why don't I transport us into his quarters?"

"I don't think so. We would probably just be killed."

As the flames grew closer, devouring everything in their path, Cathie started to scream and I had to put my hand over her mouth to stop the sound being detected. I grabbed the charm in one hand and said, rapidly:

"Lord of Love, Lord of Light,
Please listen to our present plight.
A wall of flame is in our sight,
But we must make it through to win our fight.
Help me to take Michael and Cathie through with me,
So that Zygon we can see.
If we hold hands, let us break through it,
Please dear Lord help us to do it.
And let the wearing of Dilda's charm,
Protect us all from any harm.
Make this spell safe and sound,
So, on us, it does not rebound.

Thank you, Lord for your help,
I would not ask but it is heartfelt."

So, we held hands and bravely walked through the fire together, amazed that the charm Dilda had given me and the spell had worked so well. Surprisingly, there were no guards outside Zygon's quarters as they must have left to put out the fire but I had to use my laser to blow the lock on the door. When we entered, we were glad that we had set off the bomb in the landing bay, as we found Zygon trapped by a heavy piece of steel which had obviously fallen from the ceiling. He was so wounded that he could not transport himself elsewhere and his strong powers of telepathy had faded so that he didn't know we were coming. His two hybrid children from Seta were there but were too young to be of much help. Seta was next to him snorting line after line of a white powder.

"The trapped one is Zygon and these are his hybrid children from this woman," Cathie said pointing at Zygon and then Seta.

Zygon recognised Michael but had never considered him to be a threat, as he had assumed that he would not attack his own race. Michael was pointing his gun at him but Zygon had just about managed to order one of his generals, by telepathy, to rescue him. Trying to buy time, he pleaded like a puppy,

"Please don't kill me," he said. "I will make you all millionaires and you, Michael, could be a general in my army. I will make a peaceful settlement with the human race and Earth will be a better place for everyone. Please wait. We can discuss this and you won't need to kill me."

"We don't believe you! This is for what you did to my innocent wife and an innocent friend," Michael shouted, shooting him three times in the head.

However, Michael could not bring himself to kill the two infants. I felt sorry for them as they had not yet done anything wrong, despite knowing that they had to die immediately, as they might have been able to hurt us. If our plan failed, they would certainly have grown up to avenge their father's death. So, before they could react, Cathie did it saying:

"This is revenge for nearly killing me and for the plight of the abducted teenagers."

So, they were all apparently dead except for Seta but having expected to see Amba and her children, I wanted to question her. Putting my laser to her head, she woke up to the enormity of the situation and was terrified.

"What's your name?" I inquired.

"I'm Seta," she whispered. "Please don't kill me too."

"I won't if you answer my questions," I lied. "Where's Amba and her children?"

"Amba's dead and her sons are running Fred's cocaine trade on Earth."

"Whose Fred?"

"Fred Barker was my husband and your friend has just killed him!"

For a moment I thought that we had not killed Zygon but Cathie was adamant that we had.

"Perhaps Fred Barker was Zygon's human name?" she suggested and Seta confirmed this.

"Where are Amba's sons specifically? I will kill you if you don't answer me," I inquired.

"Fred's mansion is in Colombia. It's well known to the police there but they've never been able to catch him or his sons."

Cathie confirmed that this was the truth but, as a host mother, Seta was still a threat. I knew that she would warn Amba's sons who would want to take out their revenge specifically on us. So, to protect our identities, I had to dispose of her with my laser. I used my laser not my infra-red gun because she was human. Just as Michael was about to use his powers to transport Zygon and us back to our spacecraft, the general who had been summoned, surprised us by transporting himself into the room. Before we could react, he fired a single burst from an infra-red gun into Michael's heart, saying the words:

"You traitor. Now die!"

He did not die as he was not a zygonite. There was a split-second delay while the general fumbled for his laser so I was able to kill him with my infra-red gun. Michael was still able to transport Zygon back to the hold of our ship but had been compromised by the general's shot and didn't have the strength to transport himself, Cathie and me. We took a different, shorter route back because of the fire and, this time, we were recognised as intruders and had to kill every zygonite in sight. However, we were determined that our plan would be executed and that we would escape. Eventually, we reached our ship and Michael managed to get onto the back seat. We had to open the door which meant that the ship was no longer cooched and the keeper who had been observing us, closed the inner gate so we couldn't leave.

I got out of the pilot's seat and got to the control room. Cathie covered me and our ship with fire from an automatic weapon that we had on board but was too heavy to carry around. I threatened the keeper with my weapon, commanding him to open the gate. He, eventually, pressed the switch but I had to get rid of him anyway to stop him closing it again. By then I was beginning to suffer from inhaling the smoke and thought that I would be overcome. I staggered back through the debris and just made it to our ship when someone else must have gone into the keeper's room, as the inner gate was starting to close again. We only had seconds to vacate the landing bay before the Mother Ship would break up completely, killing us all.

Cathie took the pilot's seat and, successfully, managed to flip our elliptical ship on its side and reverse at high speed through the gap in the circular, inner gate into the airlock, where she slammed on the brake. With the inner gate closed and the air pressure taking only a few seconds to equalise, the outer gate opened automatically. We passed through Earth's stratosphere into outer-space with time to spare. Cathie was the heroine of the day. I will never forget how she saved us.

While out in deep space, we detonated the alphan bomb that we had left in Zygon's quarters, blowing the remains of the Mother Ship to pieces. Zygon had been transported to the hold of our ship which we evacuated into space. Now, there could be no doubt as to whether he was dead or not. Like humans, zygonites need oxygen. In the past, when Michael had appeared to be dead, he had used his inner core strength to remain alive which had allowed Mercia to revive him. Certainly, we did not want a repetition of that with Zygon.

We headed for Alpha as Michael was in desperate need of Dilda's help. When we got there, she immediately transported him to her operating table. A scan, much like an echocardiogram, showed that he had been hit in the wall of his left ventricle and needed open heart surgery to fix the tear. We both quickly scrubbed in and Dilda gave him an anaesthetic. She opened up his rib cage and sewed over the tissue with me assisting. However, his heart went into a potentially fatal arrhythmia so she shocked him twice, getting it back into sinus rhythm. When Michael came around, he was thankfully alright but he needed to rest on Alpha for a while. Both our friendly megalattans were given a humanising depot injection and the clothes that they had arrived in.

News of Zygon's death and the destruction of the two Mother Ships spread like wildfire amongst the members of his race. The problem for them was that, just as we had thought, Zygon had been in complete control. Although he always had senior parliamentarians and generals with him, they were all terrified of him and had done everything that he had ordered them to do. They had been on both Mother ships and were now all dead so, in disarray, it was the zygonites turn to panic! All the moons disappeared with their human females overnight. Cathie told us that they had gone back to Crema which was about forty minutes away from Earth, by time travel.

With the disappearance of the moons, Earth soon became vibrant again. Power was restored by army personnel and the governments and the police returned so law and order resumed. People moved back to the cities and the world started to recover from the universal fear. Technology became available to everyone, including ordinary people, but they seemed to have more respect for it now. The stock markets re-opened and the banks were bailed out by their respective governments. However, some preferred to keep their life savings in a safe at home rather than a bank which they hadn't been able to get any money from when the moons appeared. Interest rates were increased again and inflation fell. The supermarkets were re-stocked and those that had not died of starvation could afford to buy food from them again.

We stayed on Alpha as we guessed that Zygon's two sons in Colombia would know about their father's demise and might try to find us to take revenge. Cathie contacted the organiser of the host mothers, Diana, who also knew that Zygon was dead, and gave her the information that we had gleaned from Seta. Diana passed the information on to General Howard at the White House and he spoke to the President to get permission to bomb the mansion in Colombia. The President agreed so Howard then spoke to his contact at the Pentagon, which was running again, albeit with a shortage of staff. They already knew about Fred Barker and his cocaine trade. They had the coordinates for the mansion which was conveniently isolated from other buildings in the country. A plan was hatched to bomb it with a 'stealth plane' as this would not be detected by radar.

The sons' telepathic powers were not as strong as Zygon's had been. While busily occupied in trying to find and kill us, they were unaware of the Pentagon's plans, so made no efforts to transport themselves elsewhere. The mansion and the surrounding land were bombed and the sons, the guards and their cooched ships were all destroyed. The only humans that suffered were those in the USA who were dependant on Zygon's cocaine trade. However, it severely compromised the zygonites, as Zygon's eldest son would have made a much better leader of his race than the one they eventually chose on Crema.

Diana informed Cathie that Zygon's sons had been killed and that the people on Earth were beginning to get their old lives back. I got Dilda to give me more of my inheritance to invest in my riding school. Once Michael and Sonja had fully recovered, we thanked Moma Cara and Dilda and returned to Earth.

Although time on Alpha did not count on Earth, we had been backwards and forwards to Earth while we had been away so we did not arrive forty minutes after we had left. It was more complicated than that. Pete said we'd been away for about three months and, in that time, we had changed the course of Earth's history. The moon ships had disappeared and all of Zygon's offspring had been killed.

However, the mother of one of the gang who had raided Michael's farm was still alive and went to the local police to get justice for her son. Michael was suspected of manslaughter and taken away to a police cell but we all lied and denied any wrong doing. The police had a warrant and checked over the farm. However, they could not find any evidence to support the mother's claim and, by then, all the other relatives had died of starvation so they could not be interviewed. In fact, the rest of the village protested, saying that they would have perished without the provision of free food from Michael's farm. The police, who were already over-worked, had little option but to release Michael without charging him.

Michael was pleased to find the stocks and shares he had bought at a very low price were doing well but

Rosie and Paul had not been able to buy animal feed or replenish their stocks and so his farm was in ruins. He had to go to his vault near London to collect more gold to invest in it. Despite Pete's efforts, my ponies had been stolen. It saddened me to think that they had, probably, been eaten but I used my inheritance money to buy some more. Pete was inundated with business interruption claims, something that he specialised in. David returned to the farm and Cathie continued with her post in Obstetrics & Gynaecology.

Part 7

THE TEENAGERS STORY

We will always remember planning our attack on Crema. We needed Alpha to provide us with spaceships, alphan pilots, alphan doctors and weapons to attack the zygonites and rescue the captured teenagers. If we were successful, we would also need a place on Earth for the teenagers with both medical and rehabilitation facilities. Initially, both requirements seemed impossible.

Despite Zygon's death we continued to call his race 'zygonites' as the nuclear fall-out had mutated them so that they were not typical megalattans like Michael and his family anymore. Although they had the same physical form, the adults now fed on the distress of others. Most of them had enhanced telepathic abilities which were not limited to contact with just a few in their immediate circle. As far as we were aware, all the zygonites and hybrids could be killed by infra-red weapons but would only be compromised by ordinary lasers, whereas the opposite was the case for the original breed of megalattans. Although Michael and his family all had the power of transportation to some degree, the same was not true for either the zygonites or the hybrids.

When Dilda got my message, she spoke to Moma Cara who approached the alphan High Council. There was a mixed reaction to this proposal. A significant proportion of the council did not really want to get even more involved in what was, essentially, an interplanetary war that didn't appear to have a direct bearing on their own security. However, it was the actions of the zygonites, themselves, that finally persuaded the alphan doubters to support our mission.

The zygonites were having great difficulty feeding the abducted teenagers and their young hybrid off-spring who only fed on the distress of others once they had become adults. Crema had salt water and oxygen but, as it was still in the early stages of evolution, the native life consisted of little more than inedible vegetation on land and plankton in the sea. There was nothing there to prey on and the zygonites were not natural farmers.

Like Alpha, Crema had two suns but they were in different quadrants in the sky so that it was never really dark on the surface of the planet. This was not to the liking of the zygonites who struggled with the continual exposure to infra-red light. Their scientists had developed protective clothing which resisted the intense infra-red weapons that humans had attacked them with on Earth. However, they did not like wearing it, as it was too heavy and slowed them down and they were not expecting to be attacked.

They already had buildings on Crema, as it was the planet that they had fled to when their native planet, Megalatta, had been nuked into oblivion. They had returned there to 'lick their wounds' and rebuild their moons, after they had been nuked by NATO and again more recently, when their Mother Ships on Earth had been destroyed. Only a little alteration was needed to transform the complex into a prison for the abducted girls. The smaller craft landed first but, once the buildings were ready, the moons landed and the girls, hybrids and guards were transported to their new home. The girls were chained together, in groups of five but a few escaped. However, there was nothing to eat or drink and so they soon wasted away in the desert. The zygonites transported their giant containers of negative human emotions, to feed their adults, from the moons to a large courtyard in the middle of the complex.

All of the zygonites, except the hybrids, had had a humanising depot which would last for about six months, as it was better when taking turns to impregnate their victims. This was not necessary for the hybrids as they already looked human. Males that had formed hybrid couplets were not expected to mate with the genuine humans.

Some of the zygonites even ventured back to Earth in cargo ships, to raid the supermarkets and factories. They also stole food from other planets but there was never enough to go around and some of the captured humans were slowly starving to death. In general, the hybrid infants were fed first and then the couplets, while what food remained went to the adolescents in the dungeons. The bodies of those who had died were just left to rot there, in situ.

Wisely, Dilda was concerned that the zygonites might travel to Alpha to steal stored bagaloo from the three distribution sites, as it was late autumn. So, Moma Cara limited the amount of bagaloo in the distribution sites to just what would be required for the next couple of weeks. The vast majority was left in the main undersea store, which could easily be retrieved by Dilda's magic. In addition, she issued a red alert warning so that the sites were guarded all the time.

Unfortunately, when the zygonites did attack, the guards were easily overpowered and killed and their assailants made off with the bagaloo in the stores. Initial reports suggested that the attackers were human. Fortunately, one of the assailants had been hit by a laser and had reverted to his native type so it soon became clear that it was the zygonites who had stolen some of Alpha's food.

Understandably, after that, no-one wanted to guard the stores anymore. So, one large cave was chosen for the food and manned with army soldiers with infra-red guns. When the zygonites came back, they didn't expect any resistance but they were all killed and their dead bodies were easily recognised.

I was sorry for Alpha's losses but there was a very welcome upside, as resistance to the alphas providing us with the necessary resources to mount an attack on Crema, dramatically reduced. Most of the alphas wanted this evil race destroyed. The fact that everyone knew that some of the bagaloo was being taken to feed the captured humans, who would have starved otherwise, was the only consolation.

The High Council decided to call a referendum, asking just the question of whether the alphas would provide us with the resources necessary to attack Crema, or not. They were also concerned about what should be done about Michael's megalattan family but decided to defer any decision on this, until our mission had been completed. The vote was heavily in our favour. The few that had voted against us did so because they thought our mission was impossible, that alphan pilots and doctors would be killed and spaceships lost. Dilda passed the news to me, telepathically, as we were all still on Earth.

Eventually, we commandeered eleven ships: one freighter with a hundred beds in it for those in labour, four carrier ships with two hundred seats in each hold and six small battleships that were fitted with strong infra-red light dispensers. These were attached to the bottom of the ships and electronically wired through to the dashboards in their cockpits. The battleships would all have two pilots and the others just one. All alphas going to Earth, including the eight obstetric doctors on the freighter, would have a humanising injection, lasting for about twenty-four hours. This decision was made because their alphan form may have alarmed the teenagers, as well as those waiting to receive them on Earth.

Fortunately, alphas give birth in the same way as humans so, at least in this regard, their anatomy is similar. Therefore, the alphan doctors who might have to deliver babies from the human girls did not require additional training. We would have liked some alphan medical staff on the other ships destined for Earth. In particular, there was an obvious risk that some of the human teenagers would be injured during the forthcoming battle and they might require immediate medical attention. However, as the journey from Crema to Earth would only take forty minutes when travelling so much faster than the speed of light, the High Council ruled this out. Obviously, we had to settle for the help that the alphas were prepared to give us.

As the captured girls were English-speaking and I had been born in Britain, I wrote to the British Prime Minister. I asked to talk to her in private and told her that I knew where the missing teenagers were being held and that we had a plan to rescue them. I also said that we would need facilities to look after them once they were back on Earth. She wrote back, giving me an appointment to discuss my letter. Pete came with me for moral support, as I was anxious that she wouldn't believe me.

After the formal introductions were made, we sat down in her office at No. 10.

"You had better make this brief," she said, "I have a cabinet meeting in half an hour."

"Please will you keep this meeting private and not report it to the press?" I asked initially.

"If you make any sense to me I will probably have to tell my cabinet but, I assure you, it won't be leaked to the press."

"My daughter, Cathie, is a host mother and is in telepathic contact with the zygonites. She says the abducted teenagers have been taken to a planet called Crema," I began.

"So, there is no way of rescuing them," she observed.

"I am a hybrid and am part-alphan," I bravely admitted. "The alphas have voted to allow us to have five spaceships to transport the human captives to Earth, six space battleships to kill off the zygonites and hybrids and enough explosives to blow-up their buildings on Crema."

"My information suggests that you were born on Earth and your parents Kenneth and Mary Phillips were both human, so I am curious to know how you can be part-alphan?"

"Yes, that's true but I was born on Alpha first. Mary was having IVF and my DNA was hidden and put into her harvested cells before they were fertilised by Ken's sperm. The process is called Embryolization."

143

"Why in God's name, would the alphas have done that?" she asked, completely baffled.

"I was quite an important child on Alpha. As Astra, I played a huge role in helping Alpha to defeat a megalattan army who were trying to steal all of Alpha's food. The megalattans came from the same race as the ones that have abducted Earth's teenagers. An alphan witch and traitor was ordered by their king to poison me and the Embryolization process was used to save my life."

"This is true," Pete added. "I have travelled to Alpha with my wife and, once she gets there, she naturally changes into an alphan-looking person."

"Well, I've heard of some zany stories but this beats the lot! How many other alphan hybrids do we have on Earth?" She was obviously flabbergasted but we continued to answer her questions.

"As far as I know, all the other Embryolizations failed and I'm the only one. The others were miscarried or still-born."

"I can just about accept that but I don't really understand how you both get there, except maybe in your dreams?" she asked, facetiously.

"I have a contraption called a hopper which we use to get there."

"That's true," Pete added. "And no-one can see us as it is cooched, that is hidden from sight and radar."

"I see but why can't the megalattans or zygonites stay on Crema?"

"The megalattans were mutated into zygonites who are now sensitive to infra-red light. With two suns there is too much infra-red, so it is not really suitable for them and there is nothing to feed the teenagers and the infant hybrids there. Besides, there is a real risk that they will mount another attack on Earth."

"So where did they come from originally?"

"Megalatta - but it was destroyed by a nuclear war and the fall-out mutated them into zygonites."

"And why did they want our teenagers?"

"Their females became barren because of the fall-out so they disposed of them. Believe me, Prime Minister, they are evil; they nearly destroyed the alphan race and will keep trying to destroy ours too," I replied, becoming exasperated with her obvious lack of knowledge of basic zygonite characteristics.

"I see," she said in a softer tone of voice. "Well, what do you need from me?"

"We need to care for and rehabilitate the adolescents, after we have brought them back. We need decent accommodation with beds and bathroom facilities, a means of feeding them and access to hospital treatment with trained doctors and nurses."

"You really think that your plan will work, don't you?"

"Yes, Prime Minister, and we have to act as fast as we can as there is nothing for the humans to eat on Crema and they are slowly dying of starvation. The zygonites have a means of taking human form and have been stealing food from Earth and Alpha but there's never enough. The moons only left Earth because we managed to kill their leader, Zygon. He was a psychopath, a bit like Hitler, except that he was in complete control of his race. The time is right to attack Crema as the zygonites are currently in disarray. Once they have a new leader, they could grow strong again and there is a risk that they will not only attack Earth but Alpha as well," I said, hurriedly, feeling quite pressurised by her.

"So that's the other reason why the alphas want to help us. Alright, I kind of get the picture and have some belief in you now. I will consider your plan but will have to discuss it with my cabinet."

"Thank you!" I said relieved. Then added, "Please try to keep it secret from the press. There are still host mothers on Earth and if they were to hear about our plan, they might, inadvertently, warn the zygonites who can still pick up their thoughts by telepathy."

"So, the telepathy must work both ways?"

"Yes, exactly and it has been a problem for us in the past."

The interview was concluded and she must have spoken to her cabinet who deliberated for what seemed like a long waste of time. Eventually, she sent for me. She agreed to prepare for the return of the missing humans. We estimated that at least a hundred out of the thousand girls abducted, would have died from starvation and maybe more would die in the forthcoming battle. However, we had to provide beds for them, just in case the death toll was lower than we expected. So, four warehouses were built on the land adjacent to Zygon's flats in South-East London. Altogether, they contained a total of eight hundred beds with bathroom facilities, including showers.

Zygon had actually intended to erect more flats for his people on this land but his plan had been foiled by the actions of the hybrid Daniel. The two-bedroomed flats were now empty and we were told that we could use them as well, providing another two hundred beds. We had decided that they would be suitable for the couplet girls, which meant that the girls from the dungeons would be housed together and closer to their friends.

Initially, the Prime Minister had thought that the existing hospitals in South-East London would be able to cope with the influx of women needing care but she found that they were already stretched to their limits. So, a pre-fab hospital was built on the site with a hundred beds. This included a labour ward with infra-red light boxes for the hybrid babies and two operating theatres. On the ground floor, there was an expansive kitchen with a large canteen. An area was left in the park so that the alphan ships could land but there was only enough space to accommodate one ship landing at any one time.

Paramedics and the site managers were informed and were waiting to be called to escort the girls from the ships to their new accommodation. The canteen staff, paramedics, doctors and the nurses had all volunteered to work on a temporary basis. However, the officials were paid because it was intended that they would look after the daily running of the site. Some of them would have to remain working there until all the girls had left or had been re-united with their families. They would help Cathie and Rosie with this process. So, it became general knowledge that there was a plan to rescue the girls but the details of how this was to be done and my hybrid background were kept secret.

All this activity could not be completely hidden from the media but we told them very little and said that we would talk more freely after we had succeeded. Everything on Earth was now ready for the new arrivals. At first, the British government had covered the brunt of the cost but soon money came pouring in from the other countries that had lost adolescents. It was also particularly encouraging to see some huge donations being made to the charity set up by Cathie and Rosie. All we had to do now was rescue the human captives and destroy the zygonites. It sounded simple but, clearly, it would not be that easy.

Cathie was still in telepathic contact with the zygonites and told us that there had been in-fighting over the choice of a new leader. One of the scientists, called

Astex, had reluctantly taken on the role. However, he was politically weak, had no military background and insignificant powers of telepathy. As a result, it was relatively easy for us to keep our plans hidden from him. All of the zygonites were in human form and none were wearing protective clothing. Cathie could also see a picture of the complex and with Dilda's help had drawn up a map of it.

It was built in stone and was rectangular with a main entrance or gateway in the middle of one of the shorter sides which provided access for those who could not transport themselves. There were four turrets, one in each corner so it looked rather like a medieval castle. The turrets were connected by open walkways, at first floor level. Below, there were rooms on both long sides with slightly elevated floors to allow some light into the basement. Access to these rooms was from window-lined, covered corridors that ran along the inside of the building.

Looking in from the gateway, the ground floor comprised of two hundred rooms for couplets with human females on the left-hand side. The rooms for the single male guards and hybrids of both sexes were on the right. This was important information as it might have been difficult to distinguish between the human and hybrid girls. Clearly, we did not want to make the mistake of transporting hybrids to a spaceship destined for Earth, if at all possible. Fortunately, Cathie was certain that all of the female hybrid teenagers were housed on the right-hand side. At the far end, opposite the gateway, the creche and labour rooms were on the ground floor. Kitchens and other service areas were below at basement level.

Normally, two guards were posted on the top of every turret and there were four at the gateway. The towers had no living quarters in them. All available space was designated for storage, holding useful items such as most of the anti-infra-red suits and their robots and weaponry, when not in use. All four turrets had a spiral staircase of stone steps from top to bottom. The dungeons stretched right along both long sides in the basement. The only natural light underground came from small windows which were just above ground level in the courtyard and set high on the basement corridor walls. The only light in the dungeons themselves came through peepholes in the doors.

There was a building in the middle of the large courtyard that housed the shocking machines, a meeting room and recreational area for the aliens. Surrounding the complex were the cargo ships, battleships and the moons.

The four alphan carrier ships and the freighter with the beds in its hold were all cooched and landed about a mile away from the complex. Although all alphan space craft could fire lasers, we did not want to risk losing any of these ships in the conflict. Cathie and Rosie remained on the freighter with the eight alphan doctors who were trained in obstetrics. They would administer gas and air to the women in labour once they had arrived and, if necessary, help to deliver their babies.

Michael, David, Paul and I were on one of the carrier ships but we were linked to all the spacecraft via a portable telecom and could, therefore, monitor the progress of the battle. If there was to be any change to the agreed plan of attack, then I would have to issue the orders, as I was the only one of our party who was fluent in Alphanese.

Before setting out we had spent a few hours deciding how best to attack Crema with the six battleships. All of them had powerful lasers and the newly-fitted infra-red light dispensers. It was essential that we took maximum advantage of the element of surprise, the zygonites reluctance to wear their protective suits and the fact that, while exposure to concentrated infra-red light might be uncomfortable for the humans, it was lethal to the zygonites and hybrids. It was impossible to come up with a plan that would expose the majority of the aliens to infra-red light without endangering the lives of at least some of the humans. Eventually, we had to accept the idea that even if we were only able to save the majority of the human teenagers, our efforts would be worthwhile.

First, the battleships flew slowly over the area, flooding it with extra-strong infra-red light. This killed off the outside guards and many other zygonites and hybrids who were either near the windows or came out of their quarters to see what was happening.

Then, two of our battleships fired their lasers onto the single male and hybrid quarters and the adjoining turrets which reduced the whole of that side of the complex to a smoking pile of rubble. Of course, we knew that this might injure or even kill some of the teenagers in the dungeons underneath but we just had to take that chance. Any zygonites or hybrids who survived the impact of this attack were then exposed to the continuing infra-red light field. Meanwhile, two of the remaining battleships concentrated on destroying the zygonites' moons and all their smaller ships. Although our ships could be seen when they fired, they met no resistance up to this point.

Lack of leadership was a major problem for the zygonites. Many of them would not obey Astex, as he lacked strength and conviction and they felt that he was not worthy of his role. Their judgement proved to be correct because, as soon as he had sensed danger, he had gone into hiding, in the basement service area. However, some of the zygonites did fight back.

Just when I thought that everything was going remarkably well, the zygonites sent out about twenty robots from the two remaining turrets into the courtyard. Although they couldn't see our ships, they just fired their lasers randomly into the air above the courtyard.

Despite Dilda's protective spells and the ships' cooching devices, one of our battleships, which had been helping to maintain the infra-red field, was lost in this way. It crashed into the courtyard, fortuitously crushing quite a few of the robots and catching fire but neither of the alphan pilots survived. Quickly, I ordered one of the other ships to replace it and the other three to use their lasers to destroy the rest of the robots. At this stage, some of the remaining zygonites rushed outside to put out the fire but most were killed instantly by the infra-red light.

It was time for David, Paul, Michael and I, all in human form, to move in. Michael transported us from the carrier ship to the ground floor corridor at the far end of the complex. Cautiously, we headed for the labour ward. On the way, we had to pass by the creche, where all the new-born babies and young children were being cared for. There were two guards stationed in the corridor outside who were clearly in a poor state as a result of the infra-red attack. We finished them off but didn't enter the creche itself. Once we got to the labour ward, we killed the alien midwives and I announced to the girls:

"We have come from Earth and are going to rescue you. The journey will only take about forty minutes and there will be pain relief on board the ship, with doctors to deliver your babies."

I chose the ones who were closest to delivery to be transported first, then the rest followed in small groups. Once they had all been transported to the freighter, I let the pilot know, via the telecom, and the ship left for Earth immediately.

We placed bombs in the labour ward and then outside in the corridor, then moved down towards the dungeons. We killed any remaining guards and then we opened all the doors, with the keys obtained from the dead zygonites. The stench of human urine, faeces and rotting flesh was appalling. The girls were filthy dirty and alarmed by all the noise, especially those who were under the rooms that we had already destroyed. Remarkably, most of the basement ceiling had remained intact and the girls there had escaped with just a few superficial injuries.

Again, I told them that we'd come from Earth to rescue them. They were no longer chained together but were handcuffed. We unlocked some of the handcuffs, in each section, and gave the released girls the keys, so that they could unlock the rest. Then David, Paul and Michael transported them in groups of five to the waiting carrier ships. When they had all been transported, three of the carrier ships were completely full and set out for Earth, while we placed bombs in both sets of dungeons.

I thought that finding all the couplet teenagers had to be a much more dangerous task as we did not know how many zygonites had remained in their rooms. I made sure that the infra-red light field was maintained while we did it. We were pleased to find the couplets' quarters still intact but there were about two hundred doors so we split up into two groups to save time. We didn't want to enter the rooms in case we were attacked by a male so we banged loudly on each door separately and waited for a response before moving on to the next one. If we just heard a female voice, we would transport her to the one remaining carrier ship. Fortunately, quite a few of the males had left their rooms to try and join in the fight but if a male opened the door, we would have to kill him, before transporting the girl.

This task became easier when I realised that none of the zygonites remaining in the couplets' quarters, were actually armed. When I thought about it later, it seemed obvious that the guards didn't need weapons to keep control over their partners. However, having weapons in their rooms would have put them at risk when they were asleep. While we still had to be careful to avoid giving any of the guards the chance to get close to us, the process of transporting the human girls accelerated. Eventually, I think we managed to get all the girls out.

Then a very tired Michael transported us to the remaining carrier ship. Just before leaving for Alpha, the battleships flooded the area with infra-red once more. Then, when we were all in deep space, their pilots detonated the bombs that we had hidden all over the complex. We hoped that we had destroyed the zygonites forever.

The girls and young women from the labour ward and the dungeons were all in a terrible state. Some of them were injured from fighting with the guards, lack of exercise and continual rapes. Some of them could hardly walk and most were traumatised by their experience. Not one of them was in a fit state to be re-united with their families or go to their own homes, at least not just yet. The hospital ran at full capacity and the doctors and nurses were extremely busy. Delivering all the babies and getting the adolescents clean, fed and properly clothed was a nightmare but, at least, fresh clothing had been donated by a number of charity shops.

Undoubtedly, it was the couplet girls who caused the most trouble. They were on the same ship as us. Some were in the early stages of labour and some had been transported with their babies in their arms. Others were genuinely in love with their guards and were distraught by what we had done to their partners. They were also concerned for the fate of their children and did not want to return to Earth at all. As the carrier ship took off from Crema, we had to deal with a group of angry protestors. Michael thought our safety might be at risk and transported us into the small space, behind the pilot's seat. Consequently, we had to stand for the rest of the forty-minute journey, while listening to this group of girls shouting, crying and kicking the doors of the ship.

When we landed on Earth, we did not know what to do. Some of the girls were making such a noisy protest in the hold. We assumed that all the other ships had gone back to Alpha. However, this one, with the couplet humans could not return, until the girls had been delivered and taken to their temporary accommodation. Also, it could not be cooched while the doors were open and the pilot was waiting for us to find a way to pacify the girls. So, we called the Special Police Squad, which had been set up to investigate and deal with all problems to do with the zygonites. We thought that they would be sensitive to our plight but they were fascinated by the spacecraft and started to ask awkward questions about it.

"Forget the ship for the moment. Just help us with these angry girls!" I exclaimed.

They got the girls out and handcuffed the main trouble-makers who were led to their bed areas. They were restrained by the male nurses so that they could be given sedative injections by the psychiatrists. This process had to be repeated with those that had been transported with their babies, as they became distraught and started to protest when their babies were taken away. All of those who had been injected had to be carefully monitored afterwards.

Initially, we had thought that the girls from the dungeons and the labour ward would need more urgent help and, from a physical point of view, that was definitely the case. However, in the main, they had come to accept the dreadful conditions they had endured in the dungeons. Yes, of course, it would take a lot of care over a long time for some of them to fully recover from their traumatic experience but, in the short term, most of them were grateful to have been rescued.

In contrast, most of the couplet girls were in a much better condition physically, as their treatment had not been anywhere near as grim and brutal. Some of their guards had been tender and even caring. They had been allowed to keep their babies, at least for the first couple of years until they became too strong for their human mothers. Even after that, they could have supervised visits to the creche to see their children. Seeing their loved ones killed 'in cold blood', being transported to the hold of a carrier ship and being separated from their babies had made some of them hysterical.

Three couplet girls committed suicide in the first week. One of the girls had gone down to the kitchen area and stolen a large, sharp knife and had used it to cut her carotid artery in her neck. She had died instantly. The other two had found it and followed suit. We were all sorry for the loss of these girls and it was most disheartening to have to find and inform their next of kin. The knife was taken away and the kitchen was kept locked after that. The psychiatrists were urged to concentrate on this section of the girls, especially those who were pregnant and those who had just had their babies removed.

A few of the babies delivered by the couplet girls didn't die in the infra-red boxes and were deemed to be mostly human, by the staff. However, the Supreme Court had ruled that any babies with zygonite cells in their blood, should be killed. So, I checked the babies' blood which revealed a substantial proportion of alien cells in all of them. We tried to use our lasers on them but when this failed, I decided to drown them as zygonites, like humans, need oxygen to survive. Understandably, no-one else wanted to use the physical force necessary. Although they did return to alien form once they were dead, many of the nurses were unhappy about the brutality and wouldn't talk to me for days. However, it was a necessary evil to save the human race. The last thing Earth needed was a new breed of adult hybrids that were impervious to both lasers and infra-red weapons.

I had been unable to kill Seta's children but the continual fighting must have had a very important effect on me, as all I felt, when holding the babies under water, was expediency. I wondered if I was becoming as evil as the zygonites and this worried me. Had all the killing really changed me?

When the couplet adolescents learnt that their babies had been killed and that the buildings on Crema had been destroyed and, therefore, they had lost their older children, there was a riot led by a young, couplet women, called Angela. Members of the Special Police Squad arrived to settle the protesters and take away the ringleaders. Angela was charged with causing an affray and was, eventually, sentenced to three months imprisonment.

The site managers and both my daughters were doing well with re-uniting the adolescents with their families and getting the others back to their own homes, once they were ready. Therefore, Pete and I decided to go back to Alpha to thank the alphas properly and to have a week's rest.

No-one involved in the battle could tell the alphas that the zygonites had been totally destroyed as there was no way of knowing but all of us had done our very best. There were just two problems. One of the battleships had been destroyed and the alphas had already had a period of mourning for the loss of the two alphan pilots. Also, the second carrier ship to leave Crema had not returned to Alpha, after depositing its cargo of teenagers on Earth. We were not particularly worried about the alphan pilot as we assumed that either Dilda would find him or he would return to Alpha sometime soon. To be honest, by the time we had arrived on Alpha, we had actually forgotten about him - we were far too wrapped up in the celebrations that were taking place all over the planet.

When we were invited to join in, I asked Moma Cara if I could try to get some of the dragons to come as well. I reassured her that it would be safe, so she agreed and I used a simple megalattan spell to summon some of the adults. While I was there as Astra, the dragons were very calm and peaceful. I gave the Grey a big hug when he, affectionately, bent down to nudge me with his long nose.

There were no roller coasters or mechanical playgrounds for the children on Alpha. So, the Grey and some of his adult descendants were happy to oblige by flying trips around the bay and at one point ascend into the air and breath out a little fire, before coming back in to land. Marcus and I rode on their backs, holding an alphan child in front of us and I became known as 'Astra the Dragon Lady'.

Once the celebrations were over, Moma Cara was summoned to the High Council to discuss the fate of Michael and his family because of their megalattan origin. A vote was taken and the consensus of opinion was that they should be spared. This was because they had been living on Earth peacefully, fought bravely against the zygonites and had helped the captured humans to return to Earth. However, it was made clear that if their offspring showed any signs of aggression, they should be subject to the death penalty. This decree would be overseen by Dilda. Moma Cara agreed and thanked them all on our behalf.

A day later, when I was in conversation with Dilda in her cave, she whispered to me.

"I've found an object which was one of Mercia's belongings and have been waiting to show it to you, as I think it needs an alpha to make it work. I know that I can trust you to keep it secret."

She transported me, past the security mechanism, into her small inner cave which was full of Mercia's belongings. The object was a crystal orb. I touched it and it lit up. We both looked into it and saw what Earth and Alpha would have become, if we hadn't defeated the zygonites. Zygon had made plans to kill off the entire population of humans and alphas with his nerve gas and then re-populate both worlds with hybrids. His fascist regimes would have been run by the armies, the ordinary people looked impoverished and any dissenters were being rounded up and killed. We were so glad that Michael had assassinated him.

However, there was a more disturbing prediction that the orb had to tell us, which was that we hadn't killed off all the zygonites and that there was going to be another attack on Alpha as well as Earth. I could see some figures and when I read them backwards, they gave a date when this would happen. I was disappointed and upset, bursting into tears. There was, obviously, still a threat to our existence and the sacking of Crema with the ensuing celebrations appeared to have all been in vain. Perhaps we should have made the battleships scour the zygonite complex again after the bombs had exploded but, even then, it was quite possible that some of the zygonites had not been there: perhaps mounting a raid for food, on yet another planet. The orb seemed to sense my distress and so showed me the rescued teenagers returning home and me becoming a proud grandmother with four, beautiful, peaceful grandchildren.

Meanwhile, back on Earth, there were questions to be answered about how the rescue had been accomplished. The Special Police Squad had already leaked to the press that they had seen a large spacecraft that they did not recognise. I was extremely annoyed with some of the couplet girls for causing such a fuss, after our efforts to rescue them but they were led by Angela, who had caused trouble from the start.

Britain's Prime Minister asked me to come to a private consultation with her to discuss the rescue and arrange for her to meet Alpha's Supreme Leader. Of course, this conversation was between her and me but somehow the papers were full of it the next day. At least, the fact that I was a hybrid was not leaked to the press.

The reporters were outside our house and Michael's farm. I had to apply to the High Court to get an injunction against them which was, fortunately, granted. From then on, the press were only allowed to comment when the rescued teenagers were fit enough to be returned to their families or homes. In general, the human race was grateful to the alphas and many wanted to meet them but we didn't want Alpha to be flooded with tourists, so we kept their space technology as secret as possible.

Despite this, Moma Cara agreed to see the Prime Minister but no other politicians or members of the press. So, at an arranged time, I flew into her large office, in Downing Street which had been cleared to accommodate the hopper. Pete was sitting on one of the back seats. I strapped her into the front seat and could tell that she was scared, as she was shaking and sweating profusely.

"Prime Minister, it doesn't look like much but you'll be perfectly safe as long as you can hold your breath for thirty seconds during re-entry to Alpha," I said, trying to reassure her.

"I've been on it many times now and there have never been any problems," Pete added.

From the front seat she could see the stars, even with the cover electronically pulled over us to keep us warm. Her large bag was strapped next to Pete's seat. For once, I had remembered to feed Fred and George with a box of Walkers crisps beforehand.

"You must feed us more regularly," Fred had moaned in thick alphanese. "We are more than a car that occasionally needs filling up with petrol. In case you hadn't noticed we are living creatures and need food on a regular basis!"

"I promise to be more considerate in the future," I had replied, feeling ashamed again for how often I had not thought of their needs.

We got to Alpha in twenty minutes and Moma Cara came out to greet us. Dilda was with her to act as an interpreter, as I had taught Dilda English. The Prime Minister was still slightly dazed by all the stars flying by so fast and our re-entry into Alpha's atmosphere. My instructions, on the intercom system had gone like this:

"In Earth's stratosphere, put your oxygen mask on. Flying fast through space, shut your eyes if feeling dizzy. Entering Alpha's atmosphere oxygen off, hold your breath. Now in Alpha's stratosphere, so oxygen on again. Now safe without oxygen, coming into land."

Moma Cara cooked some bagaloo. The Prime Minister asked what it was and she replied that it could be anything she liked, so she chose vegetable lasagne and was delighted with her meal. After that, she opened her bag and presented Moma Cara with a large, eighteen carat gold trophy as a means of saying thanks.

The cavens were, as always, suspicious of the stranger but their curiosity got the better of them, starting with Moma Cara's sextuplets who were introduced to her. Dilda's offspring and Moma Cara's children began to play a game, roughly translated as 'It' around us. They were totally ignored by Moma Cara and the Prime Minister who were deep in conversation, until Dilda's youngest fell over a tree root and knocked himself out.

There was a shard of broken bone coming out of his left shin and so I took over the translating, while Dilda left to treat her son.

When she returned, the Prime Minister appeared to be genuinely concerned and said, "We could hear him screaming. Is he going to be alright?"

"Thank you for asking. It was relatively easy to push the bone back into place, while he was unconscious. Then I used a bone healing injection, a solution to make the medicine work faster and a little magic. When he came around, he screamed in pain but he's now settled with a sedative and pain relief," Dilda replied.

This sparked off a conversation about Alpha's use of magic and Dilda's role as The Prime Intelligence. I was tired so went straight to bed but apparently, Moma Cara, Dilda and the Prime Minister stayed up all night, just talking. In the morning, it was time to take her back but we took her to Chequers, her country residence, this time so that she could rest. Dilda checked on her injured son before retiring and he was fast asleep but would need bed-rest for the next week.

Over the next few months, Michael, Sonja, David and Paul restored their life on their farm. Despite being pregnant with twins, Rosie continued to look after the rescued teenagers and to reunite them with their families or get them ready to go back to their homes. Cathie left the site to become a Consultant in Obstetrics & Gynaecology. She was already friendly with Alan, one of the Consultant Psychiatrists who had treated the couplet girls. They eventually, fell 'in love' and had a quiet wedding in a registry office, with a large party to celebrate afterwards.

Angela who had caused trouble from the start was out of custody by then and since she had no home to go to, she had returned to the site and had been given a flat. Immediately, she caused some of the couplet girls, who had just delivered babies, to protest and to demand the return of their offspring because they had been taken away. It didn't involve many women and the site managers were able to deal with it, without calling the Special Police Squad. They explained that their babies were now dead, as it was the law in Britain and countries all over the world, to kill off hybrids. The post-natal women soon settled but Angela wasn't satisfied.

She walked to a nearby garage and, this time, bought a container and filled it with petrol. She doused the side of one of the warehouses in the middle of the night and set fire to it with a box of matches. One official, Mark, had woken up to hear the women inside screaming, as the door had been locked for their own safety. The fire brigade came quickly and the Special Police followed. Mark was there just in time to stop Angela setting fire to another warehouse. The police arrested her on a charge of arson but, when two of the women died from severe burns and smoke inhalation, the charge was changed to murder. The warehouse was in ruins and its inhabitants were moved to the other warehouses, where there were some spare beds.

Angela protested severely about her arrest, shouting, "I hate the human race and I want them all to die!"

The families of the two dead teenagers had to be told and they started a campaign to remove all the teenagers from the site. Indirectly, this helped the managers and Rosie, especially with the girls from abroad. Pete, Rosie and I went to Angela's court hearing and she was sentenced to life with a minimum of thirty years' imprisonment. Everyone knew that she was a dangerous individual and she showed no remorse.

Later, we found out that she had made an alliance with the bullies in the prison but had had to prove herself and had been handed a knife. She had immediately attacked a poor woman who barely spoke and was depressed. Angela had stabbed her in the stomach, not killing her but making sure she would need an operation and would be hospitalised for the next few weeks.

Angela had been, temporarily, put in solitary confinement. She had received intensive counselling and I wished this had been more successful but she was so damaged by her unhappy childhood and had an extremely severe personality disorder. I don't know why I was still getting involved with her but I felt partially responsible. We had killed the only person she had ever loved and her hybrid children, brought her back to a place where she obviously didn't want to be and had not been able to help her psychologically.

However, once Angela was released from solitary confinement into the mainstream of the prison, she led a riot against the prison officers, in which she managed to hospitalise two of them. Armed police had to be called in as the protestors had climbed onto the prison roof and were throwing burning missiles at the people below. One of the policemen fired a shot above Angela's head. Thinking that he was aiming at her, she had ducked, lost her balance and fallen off to the ground below. She had broken both her legs and her back but was still alive. All the others thought she'd been shot and not wanting to risk their lives any further, quietly came down off the roof. The riot was over.

The doctors could not find any bullet wounds on her but despite their efforts, she died later in hospital. Her death was recorded as accidental and she was cremated. The only people at her funeral, apart from the vicar and a few members of the police, were Pete, myself and Rosie. I took her ashes to spread over Crema, where she had been briefly happy. I was alarmed to see signs of zygonite activity there, so I did not land but released the ashes in the air above the planet and left as soon as possible.

Part 8

ROSIE'S STORY

I will always remember the day when Paul asked us if he could marry Rosie. I thought it was a bit old-fashioned and quaint but Paul had always been polite and respectful with us and I thought that Rosie would be safe with him.

Rosie had been besotted with him from the tender age of fourteen, although I had told her that if she married him, she would have to give birth to her children at home. As well as the fact that they would look alien, for at least three months before they could be given a humanising injection. At that time no-one knew about the zygonites' vaccine but it had not deterred her anyway. She was like me in nature, shy and lacking in social confidence, but told me that she felt safe and comfortable with Paul.

Often when we visited the Woodmans, Rosie and Paul would go off for a walk together and it seemed that

Paul was crazy about her too. Strangely enough, I felt happy for them both, even though there was a huge gap in age between them. However, megalattans could live for up to two hundred years. So, if Paul was keen enough on Rosie, he could wait a few years before thinking about a sexual relationship, getting married and starting a family together. She had done a degree in Agriculture, specialising in Animal Husbandry, solely to be of help on Michael's farm.

When she had married Paul, it had been a quiet affair with only a few friends and family as she had not wanted a bigger wedding. It reminded me of my own wedding to Pete, when there were only five people there. Although we had had a large party when we got back from Barbados, Rosie didn't want this. Unlike Cathie, she never wanted to be the centre of attention and treated the wedding as if it was an ordeal to get through. She had been extremely anxious beforehand and only became calmer afterwards when she was relieved that it was all over.

She was working on the site in South-East London when she got pregnant. There were no problems with this except that she got a reptilian rash on her neck, as well as her abdomen and had to hide it all the time with a scarf. By this time the humanising vaccine, which had been used by Cathie's rapist, was available. With Cathie's telepathic information from the zygonites, Dilda had been able to make it and Rosie was given a shot, as soon as we knew she was pregnant.

She had worked at the rescue site, until her waters had broken and Paul, who was with her, had transported her back to Michael's farm. After a six-hour labour in which Michael had provided gas and air to ease the pain, she delivered two healthy babies that looked alien for a few minutes but then took on human form. So, although they were megalattan hybrids, not zygonite ones, Dilda's vaccine had worked. She could not breast-feed as she had inverted nipples, something that had bothered her ever since her early teens.

As with Bob and Beth Sanderston's adopted hybrid children, they grew up rapidly and the megalattan hybrids at the age of two looked more like human six-year olds. They could not be sent to school. Their accelerated growth rate and their special abilities of transportation of objects and themselves would have been too obviously different. The teachers would have become suspicious and then, maybe, aware of their alien origin. Consequently, Rosie was tutoring them at home. Whether it was their isolation from other children that made them misbehave, we will never know.

At the Earth age of two, they were much stronger than Rosie and, after a scolding, they would abuse her. She often turned up to see us with bruises on her face and arms. We didn't believe her when she said that she had fallen over. One day, when Paul came home from work, he found her pinned against the wall and unable to move but he said nothing about it to us, until much later. On the last occasion, they threw her against a wall, breaking her pelvis. After that, Paul had to leave his work on the farm to care for the children who were, generally, much better behaved when he was around.

One day, when he had been visiting Rosie in hospital, Pete and I were left to look after them. The children immediately threw me across the floor without any provocation. They were misogynists from the start - vicious and aggressive. Pete and I, in telepathic consultation with Dilda and, therefore, Moma Cara, decided to obey the law made by the alphan High Council. We all agreed that they had to be killed, as they would only grow up to cause all the problems that we had had before. So, knowing that they were megalattan not zygonite hybrids, I used my laser on them while they were sleeping and they died, returning to alien form. Although they were my grandchildren, I felt no emotion at all and I was still wondering about this when Paul returned.

"How could you do this to us and without consulting us first? Rosie will be devastated!" Paul shouted furiously, at me. "They were your only grandchildren. All this killing has gone to your head and you have become nothing but a murderer! You're just as cruel as the zygonites!"

"The children were aggressive, Paul, and as adults, they would have been another threat to the alphan or human races. You've got to understand that," I soothed, not entirely convinced by my own words.

"The alphas only spared your family because we promised to destroy your children, if there were signs that they would harm others and the alphas put it into law," I continued, trying desperately to defend my action.

"We're not living on your precious Alpha so why should we obey their laws?"

"Well, you're breaking the law here too."

"My father broke the law here, with the gang he murdered and you supported him then."

"Yes, well that was different as..."

"Get out, get out now! I never want to see you and Pete ever again!" he yelled.

Paul's words were reverberating in my mind. Although we didn't know each other very well, had he recognised a significant change in me? Yes, the children had seriously hurt my daughter and might repeat this but did they really have to die for their sins? Maybe their behaviour would have improved with time, like it had done for Michael, once the greedy, power-hungry, King of Megalatta? Even with these secretly hidden questions in my mind, I still felt no remorse for killing my own grandchildren and this bothered me. Had I really changed so much? Eventually, I broached the question with Pete. Although he agreed that I had seemed different to him recently, certainly harsher with people who had problems and somewhat obsessed with destroying our enemies, he fully supported my decision.

After the argument with Paul we had left immediately and returned home. A few days later he phoned to apologise for his outburst but my relationship with him remained frosty. Rosie was shown the pictures of her dead children while she was in hospital and wept for days. She could not tolerate human contraception so, eventually, agreed to a sterilization. The police were interested in the case of the two missing children and interviewed Rosie in hospital.

"I was raped by an unknown assailant and given an injection but didn't want to report it as my husband had told me that he was happy to help me bring up the children," she lied, to protect Paul's true identity.

"I gave birth when my husband was away on business and didn't realise that my babies were aliens. It was only when they got older that I noticed that they were different from normal human children," she continued, showing them the photos of her dead offspring.

"My mother, Amanda Phillips, was suspicious and killed them with an infra-red gun," she lied again.

After taking this statement and looking at the photos, the police assumed that they were zygonite hybrids. Since the law stated that all these babies and children had to be destroyed, they did not pursue their inquiries and no-one was arrested.

"I'm three months pregnant and not surprisingly Alan and I are having twins!" Cathie announced at a family dinner.

It was a day of great happiness but also great sadness as Rosie burst into tears and could not be consoled. Paul had to transport her home before either of them had finished eating their meals. For the moment, we celebrated Cathie's news by opening a bottle of champagne, although Cathie was just drinking water.

"Alan, would you talk to Rosie?" I asked, "I'm probably too close to her and was instrumental in killing off her children. You are a fresh Consultant Psychiatrist and she might open up to you. Pick a time when you feel it would be appropriate."

"Of course," Alan nodded.

When Alan reported back to me, I felt extremely guilty.

"She's clinically depressed and has been since her children were killed. Also, she is secretly jealous of her sister as she feels that Cathie is your favourite. I think it would be a good idea to reverse the sterilisation and give her another chance to have some peaceful babies. You should also spend a little more time investing in your relationship with her," he solemnly told me.

After all, Michael and his family were not violent anymore, except when it came to the zygonites and gangs that kept stealing from them. Fortunately, Rosie's fallopian tubes had only been tied with a stitch because of her young age so it was easy to reverse the sterilisation.

Six months later when I was with her alone, she announced to me, "I'm just pregnant."

"That's good news!" I replied.

Then putting my right hand on her head and Dilda's charm in my left, I said:

"Lord of Love, Lord of Light,
Listen to my present plight.
Please let it work this time,
Please let Rosie's babies be fine.
Please let them be pleasant and calm,
So, no-one around them, they will harm.
Make this safe and make it sound,
So, on us it will not rebound.
Thank you, Lord, for your help,
I would not ask but it's heartfelt."

"Was that a prayer or a spell?" Rosie asked.

"Both!" I replied.

Three months later, Cathie went into labour. The first twin's head was engaged and after ten hours, she was fully dilated and the baby was born but the second was a breech and when the midwife pulled on its legs, its heart rate dropped. The midwife reached inside and found that the cord was wrapped around its neck. She pulled it away and the second twin was born. A few months later, Rosie gave birth at home with Michael providing gas and air. Her babies looked alien at first but took on human form, after a few minutes.

Paul said to me, "Thank you for giving us a second chance!"

I replied, "That's ok. I'm glad it's worked out well for you."

However, I did wonder whether Rosie was going to be safe when her children got to the age of two years old when they would, again, be stronger than her. However, for now, I was a proud grandmother of four, beautiful grandchildren and the crystal orb had predicted that they would be peaceful, so I had high hopes. We all knew that we had broken the law again, by allowing Rosie to have children but Paul and Michael's family were extremely careful to hide their true identities. However, I did feel sorry for the couplet girls we'd rescued who'd had their babies taken away and had lost their lovers and now, finally, I could understand why they had rioted.

Once Rosie's children got to the age of two, which would be the equivalent of six in human children, we were worried that they would harm her. Thankfully, they didn't and played happily and peacefully with Cathie's children, when they visited each other. Rosie was again tutoring them at home to avoid others discovering that they were different from human children and I often helped. After what Alan had told me, I was deliberately spending more time with her and Paul and taking more interest in Michael's farm.

Then Rosie and Paul had a heated argument over their lack of money.

"I'm working as hard as I can and you know what Dad is like with money!" Paul exclaimed, slapping her hard on the face.

He had never been violent to her before and Rosie had been surprised. She had pushed him and he was going to slap her again. However, their children had witnessed the fight and lifted Paul up until he was high in the air and near to the ceiling. Without hurting them, there was nothing he could do about it. Rosie calmly helped them to get dressed and packed a holdall of clothes and accessories.

"Paul, I think we need some space for a few days. If you promise to transport me and the children to Mum's, I'll ask them to bring you down," she had said.

"I promise I'll do anything you suggest. I'm so sorry Rosie, it won't happen again!" he had frantically exclaimed.

Rosie wasn't interested in his apology but she asked the children to release him and Paul was allowed to come down, crashing in a heap on the floor. When Rosie and her children suddenly arrived at our house, my first thought was that they had harmed her as she had a bruised face. However, when she told me that Paul had done it and the children had saved her, I was astonished but believed her.

I had a spare room for her and the children to sleep in. There was a single bed in it which Cathie had used during her registration so Pete helped me to get the bunk beds down from the loft for the children. I had asked what the argument had been about but Rosie didn't want me to get involved and did not want to explain. The next day, Paul went to see Michael to ask him for a pay rise.

Michael in his megalattan way said, "Then everyone will want one."

However, once he'd heard about the recent row and how Paul and Rosie had been struggling, he gave Paul a twenty-five percent pay rise and everyone else five percent. Paul was extremely grateful and, as he had found that there was no telepathic communication between him and Rosie, he phoned my number the next day. Rosie was still hurt and not speaking to him so he told me instead and I relayed the message to her. Apart from the fact that I now knew about their financial difficulties, she was delighted but did not immediately phone him back, as she felt his behaviour had been inexcusable.

After staying a few more nights, she found it in her heart to forgive him and asked me to drive her and the children back to their home in Brockenhurst. Paul was surprised to see them but, obviously, relieved. The children were a bit wary of him, at first, but soon wanted a bedtime story from him and a cuddle. Paul promised that he would never hurt her again and, at least for the time being, she believed him.

Part 9

THE FINAL STORY

We will all remember the day when we heard on the television news that two extra, artificial moons had been seen in the sky with Davidson's infra-red telescope. It was the exact date that the crystal orb had predicted. There were two new moons over Alpha too but they nuked them without any delay. It was different on Earth and nothing was done for ages. Female adolescents from Britain were going missing again and the story was reported on the front of every newspaper. People were afraid and I requested a private interview with the Prime Minister. I urged her to get NATO to nuke these moons, as soon as possible, before we lost more teenagers and before the zygonites caused more disasters, on Earth, to feed themselves.

NATO had shown that they had the capability to send nuclear warheads to these moons but the USA had funded these before and were not willing to do it again. Certainly, not without a much more positive financial contribution from their European allies. Time was ticking on and more teenagers were going missing while the infighting in NATO continued.

The alphas had been more than generous to us and I hated asking for their help again but the alphan High Council voted to lend us two ships with nuclear capabilities. Michael and I decided that we would pilot them. While our ships could remain cooched while we got in position to attack the moon ships, we knew that they could not remain hidden while firing their rockets, so it was possible that we would be hit by enemy fire. However, we could not risk trying to enter the moons this time because, after their previous experience, the zygonites would surely be prepared for such an attack and we were much more likely than before to be recognised.

Plan A was to take out both moons and then return the ships to Alpha but we agreed on a contingency plan B. This was in case either of us were hit and one or both of the ships would not be able to make it back to Alpha. If plan B had to be activated, we hoped that we would still be able to re-enter the Earth's atmosphere without our ships breaking up and we decided to meet at set co-ordinates in the Indian Ocean. This would avoid killing any unsuspecting humans by landing on solid ground and would protect Alpha's technology.

We chose our time carefully, as we wanted to kill all the zygonites while they were on the moons. Fortunately, Davidson's telescope had revealed that the smaller, cooched spacecraft were only piercing the surface of the moons, to get in or out, during what were daylight hours in Britain. They were obviously using intermediary space craft again and I wondered what had happened to their 'captivation technique.' However, the ships could just have been carrying freight. After all the zygonites needed to steal food from Earth to feed the adolescents.

Our ships were cooched while we manoeuvred into firing positions, near the two moon ships but the cooching mechanism automatically switched off when we were about to fire. The response from both moons was immediate and both of our ships were hit by lasers. Fortunately, this did not prevent us simultaneously firing our missiles and both moons were completely destroyed. While the zygonites' laser fire did not appear to have done terminal damage, it slowed our retreat. As a consequence, both ships were caught on the fringes of the nuclear explosions which took out their main, inter-galactic propulsion systems.

We had no choice but to fall back on Plan B. As I entered the Earth's atmosphere, the intense heat in the cockpit was getting unbearable. Even though my ship was beginning to break up, I was still able to set a course for the agreed co-ordinates. I just had to hope that Michael would survive too, as otherwise I might find myself stranded in the ocean. I was still at about sixty thousand feet when I engaged the ejector seat mechanism. I parachuted down through the stratosphere with oxygen provided from small tanks, built into the seat. At about a thousand feet, I turned off the oxygen. I was delighted to be able to see Michael's parachute, gracefully, floating down a few hundred yards away.

I had never used a parachute before and was frightened for about half an hour after landing because I couldn't detach myself from it as the mechanism was jammed. So, it was threatening to drag me underwater. Yes, I had seen Michael's parachute in the sky but didn't know whether he was injured or not or whether he would be able to reach me. There was debris on fire all around me and I wished I'd used an alphanising injection beforehand as I would have been immune to the fire. I had to tread water, until Michael suddenly came up behind me. He grabbed me around the waist and kissed me on the cheek. I turned around and we kissed passionately, for about five minutes!

"I don't want to have an affair, Michael," I said clearly, once the kiss was over.

"No, neither do I. It will be our secret," he replied "I'm just so happy that we managed it and I have found you alive."

He helped me out of my parachute and transported us to my home. Pete, Cathie and Rosie had been waiting for us and had been worried sick about our venture so they were extremely pleased to see us. Michael stayed until he knew that I would be alright and then left with Rosie for their own homes. No-one ever knew about the kiss. It was our secret and we had vowed not to tell anyone. Later we travelled to Crema and found no signs of zygonite activity there. It seemed that they had put all their energy into making some smaller spacecraft and the four moons and that all of them had been on these Mother Ships, when they were nuked. Maybe at last, we were rid of them.

Unfortunately, after the attack on Crema, one of the alphan carrier ships had gone missing. The pilot had been on his own, having delivered some of the teenagers to the site in South-East London. He had taken off, heading for Alpha but had got in contact with Dilda to say that he had overwhelming chest pain and would have to find a safe place to land on Earth, as soon as possible. From the symptoms he'd described, he'd probably been suffering from a multiple heart attack. 'Multiple', because alphas have two hearts. He didn't have time to give Dilda any co-ordinates but he did say that he was aiming to land in a desert area. This would have saved his ship so he could have got back to Alpha, if and when he'd felt better and would have ensured that he would not have hurt any humans by landing on them.

He would not have been able to make an emergency landing on the site in South-East London. His ship had been the second carrier to leave Crema and there was only space on the site for one ship to land at any one time. He had, obviously, needed to land as soon as he could and was not fit enough to wait until the landing area on the site had become vacant. We had left Dilda with the task of finding him – it took many years before she finally located him, in the Arizona Desert, but the ship had remained couched, for nearly all of this time.

Michael transported us to the co-ordinates that Dilda had given us and he was able to transport what was left of the dead alpha's body back to his home. The body was badly decayed and only recognisable from the number on the ship.

"We've found him and we're determined to take him back to Alpha for his family to bury him. We're coming in Michael's buggy," I told Dilda, by telepathy.

However, when we arrived, we were greeted by a group of angry alphas. I had learnt not to expect too much from the ordinary alphan people, whereas Michael was astonished by their behaviour.

"Why wasn't he rescued before?" his brother shouted at us. "Where is his ship now?"

His wife and daughters were in tears, having expected him to come back sometime alive, after he had got over the pain. We had bought the body back in good faith, for his alphan family to bury properly, although by now he had decayed so much that he was just a bunch of bones. We could see how they felt but he had just told Dilda that he had not been well enough to travel to Alpha and intended to land in a desert, on Earth. So, she had had very little to work on.

"He didn't give Dilda his co-ordinates. It's quite amazing that she found him at all. His ship wasn't damaged and no-one had hurt him, as far as we could see," I explained.

"We couldn't use his ship because, by the time we had got there, it had run out of power. Indeed, it had become visible to the human eye when the cooching mechanism had failed." I continued. "Michael transported us to the ship and back to his farm with the body but his powers were not sufficient to transport the whole ship to a safe hiding place on Earth, let alone to Alpha."

The family were shaking their heads and the women continued to cry. They didn't seem to understand and, obviously, felt very let down by us but the brother took the body into his arms and the crowd dispersed.

We had thought that we would obtain new batteries from Alpha and travel back to the spacecraft with an alphan engineer to replace the worn-out ones. Then I could pilot the ship back to Alpha, with the engineer on board. Michael would follow in his space buggy to give me a lift home. However, before we could enact our plan, we heard from Dilda that the alphan ship, which had been cooched until the batteries ran out, had been found by the American army. They had carefully dismantled it, to remove it to a heavily guarded and safe hiding place, where they could rebuild it and learn to pilot it. Therefore, we had to give up all hope of ever retrieving it.

The spacecraft was a large, sophisticated, carrier ship that could fire lasers, enter a planet's atmosphere with the use of its shields, travel at a speed much faster than light and could be cooched, all without magic.

Now, Earth had an alien spacecraft whose technology they could copy and many humans would be able to travel long distances through time and space, without being noticed. Was this a good thing or not?

We didn't know!

Printed in the United States
By Bookmasters